Prai

Ariel

M000197368

Summer Place
...a touching romance that is genuine and timeless. The supporting players are rich and brought even more warmth and appeal to the story.

Chamomile at Whipped Cream Reviews

Out of the Fire
The deeper into the story I got, the more emotional and physical it became, and I gained a deeper understanding of the dynamics of three men enmeshed in a relationship. A Two Lips Recommended Read.

Sin at Two Lips Reviews

Hot Cargo
...definitely not your normal space adventure... it will appeal to those that like a good commanding story with some added repartee between our leading men.

Lainey at Coffee Time Romance and more

Partnership in Blood Series
This series is definitely for anyone looking for a new twist on Vampires, and who likes a bit of angst and a bit of adventure mixed into their romance.

Jaime at Dark Divas Reviews

The world building in all the books is par excellence, but in this last one, the author truly outdid herself, giving the reader a wonderful look into vampire culture. The suspense, as always, kept me on the edge of my seat and reading long into the night to find out what was going to happen.

Regina at Coffee Time Romance and more

Books by
Ariel Tachna

<u>Partnership in Blood Series</u>
Alliance in Blood
Covenant in Blood
Conflict in Blood
Reparation in Blood

A Summer Place
Out of the Fire
Seducing C.C.

with Madeleine Urban
Sutcliffe Cove

with Nicki Bennett
Hot Cargo
Checkmate
All for One

All available from
Dreamspinner Press
http://www.dreamspinnerpress.com

HER TWO DADS

ARIEL
TACHNA

Dreamspinner Press

Published by
Dreamspinner Press
4760 Preston Road
Suite 244-149
Frisco, TX 75034
http://www.dreamspinnerpress.com/

This is a work of fiction. Names, characters, places and incidents either are the product of the author's imagination or are used fictitiously, and any resemblance to actual persons, living or dead, business establishments, events or locales is entirely coincidental.

Her Two Dads
Copyright © 2010 by Ariel Tachna

Cover Design by Mara McKennen

All rights reserved. No part of this book may be reproduced or transmitted in any form or by any means, electronic or mechanical, including photocopying, recording, or by any information storage and retrieval system without the written permission of the Publisher, except where permitted by law. To request permission and all other inquiries, contact Dreamspinner Press, 4760 Preston Road, Suite 244-149, Frisco, TX 75034. http://www.dreamspinnerpress.com/

ISBN: 978-1-61581-412-1

Printed in the United States of America
First Edition
June, 2010

eBook edition available
eBook ISBN: 978-1-61581-413-8

To my daughter,
who taught me the meaning
of love at first sight.

CHAPTER ONE

"MAY I speak with Srikkanth Bhattacharya, please?"

"This is he," Srikkanth replied, not recognizing the voice.

"Mr. Bhattacharya, my name is Victoria Holmes. I'm one of the social workers at Good Samaritan Hospital. You're listed as the emergency contact for Jill Peters, and you're also listed as the father of her baby," the woman's voice continued.

"Yes, that's right," Srikkanth agreed, thinking of the arrangement he'd struck with his friend that allowed her to have a baby without having to find a man to share her life. "Is everything all right?"

"Unfortunately not," Ms. Holmes continued. "The baby was delivered this morning in perfect health, but Ms. Peters developed eclampsia, and despite the attempts to stabilize her, she didn't survive the delivery."

Srikkanth didn't know what to say. He hadn't been in love with Jill, but he *had* loved her, in that best friend sort of way. His heart clenched in his chest at the thought of her laughter, her bubbliness, her sheer enthusiasm for life and living gone. "No," he said immediately, "there must be some mistake."

The social worker knew the stages of grief as well as she knew her own name. "I'm sorry, Mr. Bhattacharya. I wish I could tell you this was a mistake, but Ms. Peters is no longer with us. We have to think about the baby now."

"The baby's okay?" Srikkanth verified, though he knew the social worker had mentioned it already. He could feel his brain shutting down already as it struggled to accept this sudden change in his reality.

"She's doing fine," she assured him, "a healthy seven pounds, eight ounces, but there are some decisions that need to be made. As the baby's father, you'll need to come in to the hospital so we can release her to you."

"No, that's not right," Srikkanth stumbled, too numb from the announcement of Jill's death to think clearly about anything else, like the bargain they'd made not to tell anyone of his paternity. "She's Jill's baby. I was only the sperm donor."

"Excuse me?" the social worker asked.

"Jill and I aren't—weren't—a couple," Srikkanth explained slowly, still feeling incredibly shell-shocked by the entire conversation. "She was a close friend, and when she wanted to have a baby but didn't have a partner, I offered to go with her to the fertility clinic and donate the sperm. She was going to raise the baby by herself."

"I see," Ms. Holmes said slowly. "Does she have family who might be interested in parenting the baby?"

"She was an only child," Srikkanth replied automatically. "Her parents died a few years ago. If she had extended family, she never mentioned them."

"Then perhaps we need to look at other options," the social worked suggested, her voice carefully neutral. "If you are indeed the baby's only relative and you have no interest in rearing her yourself, you need to arrange for her to be placed for adoption or else she'll become a ward of the state and go into the foster care system until a family can be found for her."

"I see," Srikkanth replied numbly, though he didn't see at all. These weren't supposed to be his decisions. He hadn't even figured on seeing the baby more than occasionally. He and Jill were friends, but they didn't see each other every day or even every week. Nobody else knew the baby was his—she'd steadfastly refused to reveal the father's name to their mutual acquaintances—so even if he had seen them, he wouldn't have treated her or the baby any differently than he treated any of his other friends and their kids. He didn't even know why Jill had put his name on the forms at the hospital. He'd thought she intended to be listed as the only parent of the child.

"You can't sign the termination of parental rights form until forty-eight hours after the baby was born," the social worker explained, "so you have a day to think about it. If you'd like to make an appointment, we can meet on Thursday morning to discuss your options and hopefully expedite the process so the baby can go home with a family as soon as possible."

"That's fine," Srikkanth replied automatically, not even looking at his calendar to see if he had meetings scheduled at work. This had to come first, if only so he could get it taken care of and get on with his life. "What time?"

"The baby was born at 11:41 this morning, so legally you can't sign the papers until that time on Thursday, but you could come in at eleven and we could take care of all the preliminary decisions. Since you'd be choosing voluntary adoption, you could have a say in the baby's final placement, even to the point of selecting a family for her and meeting them if you'd like."

Selecting a family. Like they were some sort of dish on a menu.

His stomach turned at the thought.

"I'll come at eleven," he agreed, "but I don't really feel qualified to make decisions for her future. I wasn't supposed to be involved in any of this."

"You don't have to be," Ms. Holmes allowed, "but if you aren't, the process is much longer for both her and you. At the very least, for a voluntary adoption, you have to select an agency to arrange a placement for her. If you don't, she'll become another case number in an overloaded system. We do our best for them, but it won't be nearly as fast as if you can bring yourself to make some decisions on her behalf."

"I'll think about it," Srikkanth promised, not sure he could commit to doing more than that.

"When you arrive at the hospital, ask for the neonatal nursery," Ms. Holmes directed. "My office is down the hall. Any of the nurses can direct you there once you get to the floor."

"Thank you for calling," Srikkanth said automatically as he disconnected the line and stared blindly at the wall.

A baby.

His baby.

She wasn't supposed to be his baby. She was Jill's baby. Except Jill, bright, funny, outgoing Jill, wasn't going to be around to raise her.

He had a friend who was adopted. Tim had met his birth mother, but all his connection was with his real parents, the people who loved him and raised him. And it wasn't like Srikkanth would be losing anything by letting her go. He hadn't planned on being more than a peripheral part of her life. This wouldn't change anything.

"Hey, Sri, are you coming down for dinner?"

"Yeah, I'll be there in a minute, Jaime," Srikkanth called back absently.

Jaime and Nathaniel, his two housemates, had already started eating when Srikkanth finally came down the stairs.

As usual, Nathaniel's nose was buried in a medical textbook as he prepared for the never-ending cycle of classes and exams that made up medical school, but Jaime looked up, surprised by the odd look on Srikkanth's face and the mechanical way he moved around the kitchen, getting a plate and serving himself without seeming to actually see what he was doing.

"Sri?"

Srikkanth didn't even look up, making Jaime frown.

"Sri?" he repeated. Still no response. "Srikkanth!"

Srikkanth looked up finally, his expression so lost and confused that Jaime wanted to give his clearly distraught friend a comforting hug. "I heard your phone ring," Jaime said instead. "Did you get some bad news?"

"I… don't even know," Srikkanth said slowly.

Jaime's frown deepened. "What's going on?"

"Apparently I'm a father," Srikkanth revealed, his voice conveying his utter confusion.

"What the hell?" Nathaniel asked, the conversation having penetrated his studying. "I thought you were gay."

"I am," Srikkanth replied immediately.

"Then how'd you end up getting some girl pregnant?"

"It wasn't like that," Srikkanth insisted. "I went with Jill to a fertility clinic to help her out. That was supposed to be the end of it."

"Did she change her mind?" Jaime asked warily.

Srikkanth shook his head. "She died."

"Oh, God, Sri, I'm sorry," Jaime said immediately. He hadn't known Jill well—it wasn't like they socialized all that much. They were housemates, and they each had their own lives—but he couldn't imagine losing a friend, especially one he'd felt close enough to to act as a sperm donor as Srikkanth had.

"Obstetrical hemorrhage?" Nathaniel asked immediately. "Or I suppose it could've been eclampsia. Or maybe amniotic fluid embolism."

"Nathaniel," Jaime interrupted sharply, "she was a person, not a case study. It doesn't matter how she died, but the fact that she did has obviously upset Sri. Just shut up if you don't have something helpful to add, okay?" He wasn't usually as impatient with

Nathaniel's unwavering focus on the medical aspect of everything—Nathaniel wasn't a bad guy, just single-minded in his determination to get through medical school and his residency at the top of his class so he'd be able to get a job and pay off his student loans—but every once in a while, his lack of sensitivity made Jaime wonder how successful he'd be with actual patient care.

Nathaniel fell silent after that, thankfully. "So what happens now?" Jaime asked finally.

"I'm supposed to meet the social worker on Thursday to decide what happens to the baby," Srikkanth replied slowly. "I wasn't supposed to be a part of this."

"You won't be," Nathaniel assured him. "You'll go in, sign a few papers, and never have to worry about it again."

"Nathaniel!" Jaime scolded. "Don't be so callous."

"What?" Nathaniel asked with a shrug that made Jaime want to hit him. "It's not like Sri was planning on raising it anyway. This doesn't change anything."

"Of course it does," Jaime disagreed. "He might not have planned on being a father, but he knew who the mother would be, and he'd get to see the baby occasionally."

"I don't have the slightest idea what to do with a baby," Srikkanth muttered, mind still reeling. "I can't possibly keep her. I wasn't supposed to be a part of this."

"Exactly," Nathaniel agreed, shooting Jaime a glare, although he tried to temper his voice to be encouraging for Srikkanth. "Go in on Thursday, sign the papers, and take comfort in the fact that you made the best decision for her and that you made a childless family very, very happy."

It made sense, Srikkanth told himself. He wouldn't have had regular contact with the baby anyway, and if he participated in the decisions, he'd at least know she was taken care of. If he abdicated his responsibility, she would end up in the system and in who knew what situation.

His thoughts jumped to his parents, back in India now that his grandparents were aging. They had pretty much given up on trying to arrange his marriage. He hadn't outright told them he was gay, but he hadn't exactly hidden it either. He hadn't ever planned on marrying or having a family, but he knew how important grandchildren were to his parents. They'd certainly lectured him enough when he was younger on his duties as the eldest son. His sister had given them a grandson the year before, which had helped some, but she was married, her family name—and the baby's—different from theirs. A granddaughter wouldn't be quite as exciting to them as a grandson would be, but it would still be a grandchild, one he'd given them. They'd fuss about him not being married to the mother, but Jill was dead. He could spin them whatever story he wanted, and they'd accept it.

Fuck. He couldn't be actually considering this. Could he? Sure, he'd win some points with his parents, but he'd have taken on a lifelong commitment without anyone to help him. And not just a commitment, but a daughter! He didn't know anything about girls, his sister notwithstanding. He'd avoided girls like the plague when he was younger because they weren't cool. And once he realized he was gay, he hadn't had a reason to get interested in them. Sure, he'd had a few female friends, Jill being the closest, but that didn't qualify him to raise a girl.

Nathaniel was right. He needed to sign the papers and forget about it.

When he looked up again, Nathaniel had already left the table.

"You all right?" Jaime asked, his dinner long since finished, but he couldn't abandon Srikkanth to his obvious turmoil. They were better friends than that.

"Would you be?" Srikkanth retorted.

"Nope," Jaime said with a shake of his head. "I'd be on the phone to my mother begging her to get over here as quickly as possible to help me out."

"You think I should keep her." It wasn't really a question.

Jaime shook his head, trying to frame his answer both truthfully and helpfully. "No, that isn't my decision to make," he said after a moment. "If she were my daughter, yes, I'd keep her, because I might not ever have another chance, but my family's here in town. I have built-in babysitters. And I helped my mother with my youngest brother and sister, so I'm not a complete stranger to babies. Adoption is certainly preferable to abortion, but even so, you rarely see Hispanic babies up for adoption because the extended family kicks in and somebody takes the child."

"The same is true in India," Srikkanth agreed, "but I don't have anyone here. They're all back in Hyderabad."

"You could take her and go home," Jaime proposed. "I know they need web designers in India too."

Srikkanth smiled sadly. "And if I did, I'd be married off to some poor girl within a month. I'm gay, Jaime. There isn't a place for me in India any more than there would be for you in Mexico. That wouldn't be fair to anyone: the baby, the girl I'd end up married to, or me."

Jaime couldn't argue with that. His parents knew he was gay, but he also knew they hadn't told his grandparents back in Mexico. He doubted his grandmother would survive the shock. He wasn't happy about the secrecy, but it wasn't like he saw them often enough for it to matter much. Nor was he seeing anyone seriously at the moment, although he had hopes for Randy, the guy he'd gone out with a few times over the past month. It wasn't like he was actually ready to introduce a guy to his family as his life partner, though, so at least for now, his grandparents could continue in blissful ignorance. That didn't help Srikkanth, though. Jaime knew what his answer would be for himself, but he couldn't impose that decision on Sri, not when this had happened so suddenly.

"Do what you think is best for everyone," Jaime said finally. "Whatever you decide, I'll support that."

Srikkanth nodded and headed back upstairs to his room, looking around the small space speculatively. The room was fine for just him, with plenty of space for his bed, dresser, computer desk, and chair, but there was hardly room for a baby's paraphernalia. He didn't have any idea how much stuff a newborn would need, but he didn't see it fitting in here. Jaime and Nathaniel each had their own rooms, but they didn't have any more extra space than Srikkanth did. Maybe even less, since he had the master bedroom. Maybe they could put some stuff in the corner of the living room, except that wasn't fair to the guys. The baby wasn't their responsibility.

She isn't yours either, a little voice reminded him.

Flopping down on the bed, he stared blindly at the ceiling, anger growing slowly at the thought that he'd gotten dragged into all this. This was Jill's baby, damn it! Yes, he'd agreed to donate the sperm, but he'd done so on the condition of anonymity, which she'd agreed to immediately. She'd told everyone she'd used a sperm donor. So why the hell hadn't she told the hospital the same thing? If she had, they wouldn't have contacted him and he wouldn't have to deal with this shit. He could just go on with his life, unbothered.

That's a lie, his conscience insisted. *You'd still know Jill was dead, even if you just read about it in the paper, and then you'd wonder what happened to the baby with no way to find out. At least this way you'll be able to make sure she's taken care of.*

Tears welled in his eyes as he thought about Jill going into labor and giving birth alone, dying surrounded only by medical personnel, with no one there to hold her hand and tell her it would be all right, even if in the end it wasn't. His thoughts raced and raced along the same unproductive vein until exhaustion finally carried him into sleep.

CHAPTER TWO

ON THURSDAY morning, Srikkanth found his way up to the neonatal nursery and to the office of Ms. Holmes without any difficulty, but he stood outside the door for a full five minutes, reminding himself of all the reasons why this was the right choice for the baby's future. None of them helped him knock on the closed door.

Finally, telling himself he wasn't helping anything by delaying, he lifted his hand and knocked.

The woman who opened the door didn't look all that much older than Srikkanth's own twenty-eight years, but her eyes were weary, suggesting she'd seen too much already in her life. She summoned a smile for him nonetheless. "Mr. Bhattacharya?"

"Yes," he said, holding out his hand. "I'm sorry I'm late."

She shook her head. "It's not a problem. Come in and we'll go over your options."

Srikkanth nodded and followed her numbly inside. This was it. He could do this. He could make these decisions and get on with his life.

The inside of the office, painted a soft charcoal grey, unlike the rest of the hospital's institutional white, was welcoming, a couch and chairs set up to provide a comfortable place to talk, with the desk unobtrusively against the back wall. He felt himself relaxing as he sank onto the couch. He could do this.

"Can I offer you something to drink?" Ms. Holmes offered. "Some coffee? A glass of water? A Coke?"

"Do you have any hot tea?" Srikkanth asked.

"Black or herbal?" Ms. Holmes inquired.

"Black, with milk, if that's not too much to ask."

"Not at all," Ms. Holmes assured him. "I'll get some from the break room."

She returned a few minutes later with a cup of steaming, milky tea. The smell of it, as familiar as his mother's perfume, settled his nerves a little more.

"How are you doing?" she asked, taking a seat across from him.

"It's all so unreal," Srikkanth admitted. "I keep expecting Jill to call and tell me it was all a mistake."

"That's a very normal reaction," the social worker assured him. "And if you were good friends—and you obviously were—it's a reaction that may take some months to fade. Unfortunately, we can't wait that long to make decisions for the baby."

"I know," Srikkanth agreed. "I feel wrong making those decisions, but I know there isn't anyone else. Can we go over my options again? I know you told me on Tuesday, but everything from that conversation is a little blurred in my head."

"Of course," Ms. Holmes replied. "For a voluntary adoption you'll need to choose an agency to handle the placement and then you'll need to decide how involved you want to be beyond that. Voluntary adoptions range from completely open with birth parents getting regular updates and even visits to completely closed with no contact at all. The norm is usually somewhere in the middle."

"I'm not really prepared to meet anyone," Srikkanth said quickly. "As I told you before, I wasn't planning on having any contact with the baby as her father. Jill and I were friends, so I'd have seen her occasionally, but that's all."

"That's entirely your choice," Ms. Holmes assured him. "The adoptive parents certainly have their preferences, but we generally go with the more restrictive option if there's a difference of opinion on the degree of openness."

She handed Srikkanth a list of agencies. "The first step will be to pick an agency."

Srikkanth skimmed down the list of agencies, finally settling on one. "I'll go with Catholic Charities," he said slowly. "The nuns do some fabulous work in my hometown."

"I'll contact Catholic Charities in a moment, then," she said. "While I'm doing that, here's a questionnaire for you to fill out to help guide your placement choices."

"They don't just give her to the next family on the list?" Srikkanth asked helplessly.

"Not anymore," Ms. Holmes said with a chuckle. "They want to make the birth parents as comfortable with their decision as possible."

Srikkanth sighed and stared at the questionnaire, with options for race and education and family size. He shook his head. "I don't know, all right?" he said, his frustration growing along with his sense of helplessness. He checked all the options for race because the baby was mixed to begin with, and even if she weren't, race was a question of skin color, nothing more. He wanted the baby to have reasonably well-educated parents so they would value education for her, but he knew that wasn't any guarantee in either direction. Nathaniel's parents hadn't graduated from high school, but they made absolutely sure he did and had pushed him to excel even beyond that. They couldn't help him pay for medical school, but they encouraged him to find ways to finance his education so he could escape the paycheck-to-paycheck lifestyle they'd struggled with their entire lives. Having grown up with a sister, Srikkanth knew the value and the frustration of siblings, but a part of him felt like he ought to give the baby to a couple who hadn't had the chance to be parents yet rather than to someone who did, except a family who already had children would know how to take care of a baby.

He hated the indecisiveness he was feeling, hated the entire situation. These weren't his decisions to make, damn it. He wanted to beat his head against the wall, but it wouldn't help, so he simply left the options blank.

"Would… would it be all right if I saw the baby?" Srikkanth asked in a rush, the words out before he knew for sure he would make the request. "It might feel more real if I can see who I'm making these decisions for."

"She's your daughter," Ms. Holmes reminded him. "You have every right to see her, although it may make it harder for you to sign the papers."

"I just want to see her," Srikkanth insisted. "I need to see if she looks like Jill."

Ms. Holmes looked like she wanted to caution him again, but she didn't, leading him down the hall to the nursery. "You'll need to wash up and put a hospital gown on over your street clothes," she explained. "Your baby's healthy, but not all the babies are as fortunate, so they're relatively strict about hygiene. Leave your jacket here. You'll be more comfortable without it on."

Srikkanth nodded, stripping off his jacket and hanging it over the arm of his chair, and followed Ms. Holmes down the hall to the entrance to the neonatal nursery. He stopped at the sink, scrubbing his hands and arms up to his elbows as directed by the placard above the basin. Ms. Holmes gestured to the hospital gowns hanging by the door as she began her own washing ritual. Srikkanth put one on over his shirt and tie and waited for her to finish up. She led him into the nursery and over to a bed marked simply "Peters, girl."

"Sophie," he said immediately, unable to ignore the pang at seeing that the baby didn't even have a name. "Her name is supposed to be Sophie."

"I'll make a note of it in her file," Ms. Holmes offered, "but ultimately, her name will be up to her adoptive parents, although we encourage them to take the birth parents' wishes into account. Often, they'll use the birth name as a middle name."

Srikkanth stroked the smooth beige skin, noticing how much darker she was than any of the other babies in the room, all of whom had about the same coloration as the white blankets swaddling them. She squirmed under his touch, her little hand lifting to brush his fingers as her eyelashes fluttered softly. "She's a darling baby," one of the nurses said, coming over to Srikkanth's side. "She eats like a horse and never fusses."

Srikkanth smiled. "She sounds just like her mother, then."

"Here," the nurse said, scooping the baby up with the ease of years of practice. "Have a seat there and you can hold her."

Srikkanth knew that was a bad idea even before he saw the frown on Ms. Holmes's face, but he couldn't resist. Just once, he told himself. He'd hold her this once and then he'd go back and sign the papers and be done with it. He took the seat the nurse indicated and tried to position his arms the way hers were so they formed a cradle for the baby. "Just support her head and she'll be fine," the nurse assured him, placing the baby gently in his embrace.

Her eyes opened as she went from confident hands to more hesitant ones, blinking owlishly up at Srikkanth. "Hi," he said softly, vaguely remembering his mother telling a young friend that she should talk to her baby all the time as if he could understand her. "How are you, Sophie? I'm Srikkanth. I'm a friend of your mama's."

His voice caught, but he swallowed around the lump in his throat and went on. "We've known each other since middle school. She was the only person who didn't make fun of the kid with the funny accent, and she had words with anyone who dared say anything about it where she could hear them. She loved Indian food, you see," he confided, "and since I was from India, she figured becoming my friend was the perfect way to steal all my mother's recipes. She could cook even then. My mother loved her. Every time Jill would come to visit, she'd follow Mā into the kitchen and watch her cook. It didn't matter to her that Mā didn't follow a recipe. Your mama just watched and learned, and then the next time I'd go over to her house, she'd prepare the recipe she'd learned from Mā. She was my first friend here in the States, my best friend."

The baby watched him with that serious expression all newborns have, the one that says they're trying to make sense of this strange new world and not quite succeeding. Srikkanth bent and placed a tender kiss on her forehead as he continued to reminisce. "Everybody thought we were dating, but Jill never pressured me that way. I think she knew I was gay before I did, and when I finally came out, she supported me one hundred percent. We got an apartment together in college, and I think my parents kept expecting me to announce our engagement or something. They don't know about me, you see. I don't think they'd understand. Jill did, though. We'd go out together and agree on the cutest guys in the club. Then we'd figure out if they were gay or straight so we could decide who got to hit on them."

He laughed softly. "I guess I shouldn't be telling you these things, but you deserve to know who your mama was before you go to another family and a different mama and daddy who can take care of you now that your mama's gone. You look just like her, you know. Sure, you got my coloring, but the shape of your eyes and mouth, they're exactly like hers. And I'll bet you'll have the same curly hair she had too. It'll be brown, probably, since her red hair is a recessive trait, but you'll get her curls. You have to. You're too much like her not to get that too."

He lifted the baby so he could rub his cheek over her smooth scalp, taking in the fragrance of lotion and soap and baby. His eyes teared up as he rocked her. "She wanted a baby so much," he whispered, "but she couldn't find a man she loved enough to marry. We'd always joked we'd be perfect for each other if it weren't for the whole gay thing, so when she got tired of waiting for the right man and decided to have a baby on her own, I was the logical person to approach. I didn't say yes right away. I was actually a little freaked out by the whole idea at first. I mean, what did I know about being a father, but she assured me over and over that she wasn't asking me to do anything except provide the genetic material. She'd take care of you on her own. She'd raise you and love you enough for two parents and four grandparents and a whole slew of aunts and uncles. And she would have. When she found out she was pregnant, she was over the moon. I've never seen her as happy as she was while she was pregnant with you. She never complained, not about the morning sickness or the clothes that didn't fit or about the swollen ankles or anything else. She spent weeks poring over paint swatches and border patterns to get everything picked out for your nursery, and then she inveigled all her friends to help her get it all set up. Everything was going to be perfect for her little angel. Only now she's not here to make it that way, and I can't take her place. I don't know how."

He rocked the baby a little closer and wept against her tiny shoulder for the loss of his best friend, soft sobs escaping his throat as they sat there. Her little hand patted the side of his face, and his heart skipped a beat, a sudden, unexpected, overwhelming wave of love stealing his breath. He lifted his head and stared down at her trusting, open face and knew he was lost.

"It's time for her to eat," the nurse said quietly, coming back to Srikkanth's side. "Her bottle's all ready. All you have to do it give it to her."

"I don't know how," he said for what felt like the thousandth time since he'd learned of Jill's death.

"It's easy," the nurse said, handing him the bottle. "Just put the nipple in her mouth and make sure there isn't any air up against it. She'll do the rest. When she's taken about a third of the bottle, call me and I'll come help you burp her."

Srikkanth nodded mechanically, tipping the bottle up and placing the teat against the baby's lips. They parted immediately, sucking on the plastic nipple voraciously. "You were hungry, weren't you, Sophie?" he asked as she ate. "I'm sorry I didn't realize. You see what I mean about not knowing what to do. How am I supposed to take care of you when I don't even know when you're hungry? You'd be so much better off with people who know something about babies."

Sophie simply kept sucking on her bottle, sublimely unaware of the conflict going on inside the man holding her. When the bottle was about a third empty, Srikkanth looked around for the nurse, who came as soon as he caught her eye.

"Work the bottle out of her mouth and lift her to your shoulder," the nurse directed. "Pat her back firmly until she burps. If you get the air bubbles out a little at a time, she can keep on drinking. If they build up, she'll end up spitting up half of what she ate."

Srikkanth patted Sophie's back tentatively.

"Not like that," the nurse laughed, giving the baby a firm thump on the back. "As long as you support her head, you won't hurt her. Go ahead; you can pat her harder than that."

Hesitantly, Srikkanth did as the nurse directed, patting a little more firmly until Sophie let out a satisfied belch.

"Now give her another third, burp her again, and let her finish the bottle," the nurse said. "You're doing fine. You're a natural as a father."

The tears sprang to Srikkanth's eyes as the nurse walked away again. He offered the bottle to Sophie again and stared down at her crinkled face, trying to reconcile his feelings with his intentions. It was an effort doomed to failure. Ms. Holmes had been right, he supposed, but he found he didn't regret asking to see Sophie.

"I can't do it," he said, looking up at the social worker who hovered nearby. "I can't sign the papers. I'm sorry."

Ms. Holmes nodded. "That's your choice. You'll need a car seat to take her home in."

Srikkanth felt his eyes grow wide, but he'd made his decision. Now he had to follow through. "I'll need a day or two to make the arrangements. Obviously I wasn't planning on this."

"She can stay here for a few more days until you can get what you need," Ms. Holmes assured him. "I'll leave you to bond with your daughter. Congratulations, Mr. Bhattacharya. She's a beautiful little girl."

Srikkanth stared down at the baby.

His daughter.

Oh, God, what had he done?

Chapter Three

SRIKKANTH had no sense of the passage of time as he sat there and rocked Sophie, crooning the same lullabies his mother had sung to him. He gave her a second bottle and watched in bemusement as the nurse changed her diaper. He reached for her again, but his stomach rumbled so loudly the nurse frowned at him. "Go get something to eat and get your car seat for her. She's ready to go home as soon as you're ready to take her."

"I… it'll be a day or two," Srikkanth apologized. "I wasn't planning on her being mine, so I don't have anything ready for her."

The nurse smiled. "A quick trip to Babies Я Us will take care of that. Get a good car seat and stroller, a selection of bottles, formula, diapers, a couple of blankets, a few pairs of pajamas, and somewhere for her to sleep. Everything else can wait until later."

Everything else. Srikkanth had a sinking feeling he was in over his head, but he'd made his decision now, and he intended to stick to it.

He just had to tell Jaime and Nathaniel.

"HOW did it go?" Jaime asked sympathetically when Srikkanth got home.

"Um," Srikkanth hesitated, "I couldn't do it. I couldn't give her up."

"You're crazy, man," Nathaniel declared, turning back toward his room. "Good luck. You're gonna need it."

"Don't listen to him," Jaime insisted with a scowl for Nathaniel. "Yes, it'll be some work, but I'll help even if Nathaniel won't. I helped my mama with my little brother and sister. I know a little bit about babies."

"They want me to bring her home as soon as possible, and I don't have the first idea what she needs."

"I don't know all that much beyond the obvious, but I know where we can figure it out. There's a Babies Я Us in the mall. We'll find what we need there, and hopefully people who can tell us what we've forgotten."

Srikkanth looked at Jaime in abject gratitude. "I don't know how to thank you."

Jaime grinned. "By letting me spoil her. Have you decided on a name?"

"Jill wanted to call her Sophie," Srikkanth confided.

"That's a lovely name. Get your keys. We'll take your car so maybe they can help us install the car seat."

Srikkanth got his keys and wallet and followed Jaime out the door. "Do you think it would be selfish of me to give her an Indian name as well? It might make it easier for my parents to accept."

"I don't think it's selfish at all," Jaime exclaimed. "Whatever your original arrangement with Jill, you're in the picture now. You're her father and you're the one raising her. I don't think anyone would even question it if you used Sophie as her middle name and an Indian name first."

Srikkanth shook his head. "Indian names are hard for people to say and spell. It's enough for it to be her middle name."

"Do you have something in mind?" Jaime asked.

"I was thinking about Thanaa. It means thankfulness," Srikkanth mused.

"I think that's a very appropriate name," Jaime agreed as they drove toward the mall. He pulled out his PDA and started typing. "We'll need bottles," he said aloud as he made a list. "We'll also need a bassinet and a rocking chair, a car seat, diapers, blankets, clothes, formula. What kind of formula did they give her at the hospital?"

"I have no idea," Srikkanth replied helplessly. "They just gave me the bottle."

"Call the social worker back," Jaime proposed. "She can tell you, or she can find out if she doesn't already know."

"I'll call her when we get to the store," Srikkanth agreed, the sense of unreality surging again at the thought of two gay men shopping for baby essentials.

"She'll need a rattle or two, oh, and a teddy bear. She has to have a stuffed animal," Jaime exclaimed.

Srikkanth whimpered, totally ill at ease.

"It's all right, Sri," Jaime said soothingly. "Just trust me."

"I'm trying," Srikkanth said, "but I keep wondering if I've made a mistake."

"What does your heart tell you?" Jaime asked seriously.

"That she's my daughter and I love her already."

"Then you aren't making a mistake," Jaime assured him. "I mean, I'm sure you'll make plenty—all parents do—but you're not making a mistake in keeping her."

Srikkanth let that sink in the rest of the way to the store. When he'd parked and they went inside, Srikkanth felt all his panic return at the sight of the incredible variety of paraphernalia to choose from.

"Relax," Jaime said before Srikkanth could flee. "One thing at a time. Let's start with the feeding supplies. You won't want to wash her bottle every time she uses it, so you'll want to get ten or twelve, probably."

Srikkanth looked at the wall of bottles and nipples and brushes and shuddered. "How am I supposed to choose?"

Jaime didn't have an immediate answer, but a woman with an infant in a sling arrived at that moment, picking out a couple of packages of nipples. "Excuse me," he said, drawing her attention. "Could you take pity on a couple of bachelors and tell us what kind of bottle you use?"

The woman looked surprised, but she picked up a package and handed it to them. "These are the ones I use, the AVENT ones," she said. "They're BPA-free, so you don't have to worry about anything getting in the milk from them, and supposedly they help reduce colic. I tried a different brand at first, but my son had terrible colic. Switching to the AVENT bottles definitely helped, although he still gets it sometimes."

"Thanks," Srikkanth said, looking at the package.

"How old is the baby?" the mother asked.

"She's two days old," Srikkanth replied.

"Then you'll want the newborn nipples," she told them. "Anything else will choke her because the milk comes out too fast."

"Thank you again," Jaime said, grabbing several sets of the nipples that matched the bottles and a bottle warmer from the bottom shelf.

"She won't need plates or cups or anything for a few months," Jaime told Srikkanth. "We can come back for those when she's older. Let's see." He led Srikkanth past the rest of the feeding supplies to the bathtubs. "Do you want to get a tub for her? Or just bathe her in the sink? That's what my mama did until we were old enough to sit up on our own, but I don't know what Nathaniel would say."

"I'd better get a bathtub," Srikkanth sighed. "I can keep it in the upstairs bathroom so it won't be in Nathaniel's way."

Jaime nodded. "Here, see the Safety 1st one? It even tells you if the water's too hot. You don't want to scald her accidentally."

Srikkanth put the tub Jaime indicated in the cart and started down the aisle.

"Do you need any help finding anything?" an employee asked, coming up to where they stood.

Finding things? Srikkanth thought. *How about knowing what to look for?* Fortunately, Jaime answered for him. "Honestly, we need help with everything. Srikkanth found out today he's a father and so we need to set up the basics of a nursery immediately."

"And we're kind of limited on space," Srikkanth added.

To her credit, the employee—her nametag read Tricia—didn't blink. "Let's try this," she suggested. "Let's get a registry and we can use that as a way to make sure we don't miss anything. There might be things you decide not to buy or to get later, but that way you'll have made a choice rather than forgetting something."

"Thank you," Srikkanth said, his voice conveying his relief.

"It's not a problem at all," she assured them. "That's why I'm here." She disappeared for a minute, coming back with a sheaf of papers. "Okay, I see you've gotten the bottles taken care of. How old is the baby?"

"She's two days old," Srikkanth replied.

"Then you probably don't need a high chair yet," Tricia mused, "especially if space is a concern. Unless you want one that reclines to have a place to put her while you're cooking?"

"I think we'd better wait on that," Srikkanth demurred.

"I'll watch her if it's your night to cook," Jaime offered.

Srikkanth shot him a grateful smile.

"Okay, on to safety gear then," Tricia proposed. "Car seat?"

Srikkanth shook his head. "All I have is what's already in the cart. She was supposed to live with her mother, but Jill died."

"I'm sorry to hear that," Tricia sympathized. "Your best bet is probably a car seat stroller combination. The car seat is good for a year or so, and you can continue to use the stroller even after that. The other option is a convertible car seat and then a separate stroller. You just have to make sure you choose a stroller that's safe for a small infant without the car seat."

"Which one is better?" Srikkanth asked.

"It's really six of one, half dozen of the other," Tricia replied. "The convertible ones are more expensive up front, but you only have to buy one rather than two or even three, including a booster seat for when she's four and older, but the sets are nice because the car seat lifts out of the base and goes into the stroller so you're not constantly having to take her in and out."

"What do you think?" Srikkanth asked Jaime.

Jaime grinned at him. "I don't know any better than you do."

"I think I'd be worried about dropping her or not protecting her head enough if I was always having to get her in and out. I guess I should go with a set."

"They're over here," Tricia said, leading them over to a wall full of options.

"Oh, God," Srikkanth groaned.

"Don't panic," Tricia and Jaime said at the same time, the ensuing laughter breaking the tension that had grown steadily in Srikkanth's belly.

"The strollers come in two basic kinds," Tricia explained. "Regular and sport. If you like to run and want to take the baby with you, the sport model is more practical. Otherwise, it's a question of fabric and price. We can't sell them if they don't meet safety standards."

"I don't want anything too frilly," Srikkanth said immediately.

"What about this one?" Jaime proposed. "The green and polka dots aren't too princessy."

"That one's very popular," Tricia agreed, "and it's got some little extras, like a place to keep wipes build right into the handle, that a lot of parents find very useful. Evenflo is a very reliable brand."

"I guess I'll get one of those, then," Srikkanth said.

"Get the one you want," Jaime insisted. "Sophie's your daughter. I'm just here for moral support."

"No, I like it," Srikkanth insisted. "I'm back to feeling overwhelmed again. That's all."

Jaime patted Srikkanth's shoulder encouragingly. "Let's get this done so you can go back to the hospital and cuddle your daughter. It'll all make sense again when you have her back in your arms."

Srikkanth nodded. "What next?" he asked Tricia.

"You'll want something to carry all her supplies in when you take her out," Tricia said. "We have a whole line of diaper bags for dads that aren't feminine, including some from various universities if you want to tout your alma mater."

"I'm not that big a fan of University of Houston," Srikkanth said with a shake of his head. "Something simple and easy to keep clean is all I need."

"Okay," Tricia agreed. "Would you rather a backpack style or a gym bag style?"

"Backpack, I think," Srikkanth decided.

"Great," Tricia said, showing them a wall of bags. "There's the Daddys Matter sling bags or the Timberland ones. Timberland is a little less expensive, but other than that, they're pretty comparable. You're welcome to take them down and look at them, try them on, whatever."

Srikkanth tried them both on, deciding he liked the ability to swing the sling bag to the front so he could get to the contents without taking it off. He added that to the growing pile in the cart. He could keep the stroller and car seat in his car and the bathtub in the upstairs bathroom he and Jaime shared so Nathaniel wouldn't be bothered by it. "She needs somewhere to sleep, and space is an issue. Her bed has to fit in my room."

"You can go with a bassinet or a cradle," Tricia told Srikkanth, "which definitely takes up less space than a full-sized crib, but she's going to outgrow it by six or seven months when she starts rolling over and pulling up, because the mattress height isn't adjustable on most of them, and even on the ones that are, the sides aren't as high."

Srikkanth sighed. "So I can either buy something small now and replace it in six months or get the bigger crib and deal with being crowded."

"Pretty much," Tricia agreed with a wry smile. "Unless you wanted to go with something like a playpen. A lot of them have two levels so you could adjust it, and they fold up and are easy to move around the house. It's not quite as nice as a bed, but it definitely takes up less space, and if you reach the point where you want to get her a crib or a toddler bed, you can still use the playpen to keep her confined, say, in the kitchen or out in the yard. In fact, we just got a new one in by Graco that might be perfect for you."

She led them toward the play yards and showed them a playpen with an adjustable bottom, a removable changing table, and a small bassinet that attached to the sides. "She can use the bassinet right now, and then when she gets a little bigger, she can sleep on the floor of the playpen, either at this height or at the lower one. The floor is nicely padded, so it's firm but not hard."

"And it isn't frou frou," Jaime teased.

Srikkanth flushed slightly. "You know how Jill was. She wouldn't want me to raise a prissy girl."

"No," Jaime agreed, sobering, "she wouldn't. She'd approve of what you're choosing."

"Okay, blankets, a couple of outfits, diapers, and formula, and I think you'll have enough to get started," Tricia declared.

"And a teddy bear," Srikkanth teased Jaime in turn. "This pushover insists she needs a stuffed animal."

Tricia laughed. "She probably won't even notice it until she's a couple of months old. Lights and music are much more likely to draw her attention, but I'll show you where the toys are and you can pick what you want."

"I forgot to ask what kind of formula she was getting at the hospital," Srikkanth remembered.

"Which hospital?" Tricia asked.

"Good Sam."

"Probably Enfamil, then," Tricia said. "That's what they use unless there's an allergy, but you'll want to make sure. Formula is one of the few things you can't exchange—for safety reasons, obviously."

"I'd better call," Srikkanth mused.

"Or wait and come back," Tricia suggested. "They usually give you enough to last a few days. That way, you'll know for sure."

"Okay," Srikkanth decided. He could always pick it up at the grocery store or ask Jaime to. "So diapers, blankets, and clothes."

"You can probably just get some sleepers, since it's still cold outside," Tricia counseled. "The dresses are cute and all, but not terribly practical when the temperatures are this low. Figure she'll go through at least three outfits a day and then decide how often you want to do laundry."

"Three?" Srikkanth echoed.

Tricia nodded. "By the time she's done spitting up and having diaper leaks, three is a minimum for the first few months. A bib will help with some of the spitting up, but again, given how cold it is, you don't want her skin to get chilled or chapped by wet clothing."

Srikkanth flinched a little. "Okay, I guess I need to get a dozen sleepers. I can do laundry twice a week, but not much more than that with my schedule the way it is." He picked out four three-packs and added them to the cart. The blankets were on a display nearby, so he grabbed four of those too. "Will that be enough?"

"Get a couple more," Tricia encouraged. "She's as likely to make a mess on her blanket as her clothes."

Srikkanth did as she said.

"Okay, diapers are in the back and the toys are near checkout, and then I think you're ready to go."

"Thank you again so much for your help," Srikkanth repeated. "I don't think I ever would've gotten done without it."

Tricia smiled. "Good luck with the baby, and don't hesitate to come back if you need something else or even if you just have questions. We do everything we can to make the store baby and family friendly."

"You've definitely succeeded today," Jaime chimed in. "Go get diapers, Sri. I'm going to get her a couple of toys and I'll meet you in the front."

Srikkanth pushed the cart in the direction of the diapers, buying a big case on the theory that he'd use them and it would be easier to buy them now when he didn't have Sophie with him. He met Jaime near the cashiers and shook his head at the pile of toys in his friend's arms. Rattles, a stuffed rabbit, a set of plastic keys, and a package of pacifiers.

"What?" Jaime asked defensively. "Everything you got for her was practical. I wanted her to have something fun too."

"You're going to spoil her rotten."

"No such thing," Jaime insisted. "She'll be happy and know she's loved, and there's no greater gift than that."

Srikkanth couldn't argue with that, so he didn't try, simply getting in line and trying not to blanch when the cashier read him the total. Sophie was worth it, he reminded himself, and he could afford it.

As they drove back toward home, Jaime broached another subject. "Have you thought about daycare? Obviously you'll want to stay home with her for a couple of months, but eventually you'll have to go back to work."

Srikkanth sighed again. "I can take up to twelve weeks with FMLA. I thought I'd take all of that first, and that'll give me time to figure out what I want to do next. I know there are a lot of really good daycares out there, but a part of me keeps throwing up all the horror stories, even knowing those are the exceptions, not the rule."

"Yeah," Jaime agreed. "Mamá didn't work until we were all old enough to start school. When my younger brother and sister surprised us several years later, one of my aunts watched them while she was at work. You have some time to figure it out. Let's get this stuff home and set up so Sophie can come home tomorrow."

CHAPTER FOUR

"LET'S get all this inside and unpacked," Jaime said when they got back to the condo they shared. "We'll see what time it is, and maybe you can even bring Sophie home tonight."

Srikkanth felt his heart leap and his stomach fall at the thought. "I think I'd better wait until tomorrow," he told Jaime. "It's already four, and we don't have anything ready, and by the time I get to the hospital, it'll be late and—"

"Relax, Sri; it's your choice," Jaime interrupted. "Let's get everything inside and unpacked and then you can decide. And if you'd rather wait until tomorrow, that's fine."

"I still have to set up my leave too," Srikkanth reminded him. "I should actually do that first, even before we set up the nursery, so I can catch the human resources people before they leave for the day."

"Good thought," Jaime agreed. "You don't want to have to mess with that hassle once you've brought Sophie home. You'll want to focus entirely on her for awhile. Do you want me to carry stuff in while you're taking care of that? I can even put her clothes in the laundry. I have some things that need to be washed too."

"You're sure you don't mind?" Srikkanth verified. "I don't want to take advantage of you."

"I don't mind at all," Jaime promised. "I have to do a load anyway, and the blankets and sleepers won't take up that much space. Although maybe I should wash the cover for the bassinet too. What do you think?"

"Yes, probably," Srikkanth mused. "Are you sure that's not too much trouble?"

"Go make your phone call," Jaime insisted. "I'll do laundry."

"Thank you," Srikkanth said as he headed upstairs to his room to argue with human resources. He knew it wouldn't be an easy explanation, but he didn't expect the conversation to take a full hour of explaining and reiterating and insisting. The company had to give him the time off—he remembered that from when the law passed—but apparently they didn't have to make it easy.

Finally, they agreed to fax the paperwork to the hospital so it could be filled out. He would have to either continue working until it was processed, however, or take vacation days until the paperwork went through.

"Fine," Srikkanth snapped. "If that's the case, then get it set up to use my vacation. I simply want to bring my daughter home from the hospital."

He resisted slamming the phone down as he hung up, reminding himself it wasn't the woman's fault Jill had died, leaving him in this unplanned situation. If he'd known ahead of time, if they'd been a couple and he'd had months to plan, he would have completed all the paperwork ahead of time, but none of this had been planned.

Taking a deep breath, he closed his eyes and summoned the image of Sophie sleeping in his arms as she'd done that morning. That alone settled his nerves. Taking a second deep breath, he opened them again and went down to see if Jaime wanted to help him make sense of setting up the playpen. He had a feeling he'd need it.

AN HOUR later, baby bed assembled, Srikkanth leaned against the side of his mattress from his place on the floor and grinned at Jaime. "We make a pretty good team."

"We do," Jaime agreed, returning the smile. "Now we have to see how we do when Sophie actually gets here and we have to worry about more than how to put together a bed. And that means we should go figure out the car seat. She can't come home if we can't get the car seat installed."

The car seat was easier than the bed, the latch system attaching to Srikkanth's car with three quick snaps and two pulled straps. Srikkanth was tempted to go back to the hospital to see Sophie even though he knew it was too late to bring her home, but after some debate, he decided to stay home and finish unpacking and organizing everything. With Jaime's help, he emptied a bookshelf, packing the contents away so he'd have a place to store Sophie's empty bottles, her diaper bag, and all the rest of her paraphernalia. When everything was as prepared for her arrival as they could make it, Jaime went downstairs to watch TV, leaving Srikkanth to stare at the baby bed and bookshelf and wonder again at how his life had changed.

He trailed his fingers over the edge of the playpen, trying to imagine the infant he had held that morning sleeping quietly in the bassinet, but his imagination failed him. He crossed to the shelf, picking up one of the rattles Jaime had bought. He shook it experimentally, trying to imagine Sophie's little hand picking it up and shaking it, her laughter filling the room as she played. He didn't know much about babies, but he did know not to expect that to happen right away. It wouldn't be long, though, just a few months, before she'd be interacting more with the world, playing with toys, snuggling with her teddy bear. Srikkanth picked it up off the shelf, rubbing the soft velour against his face. Tears sprang to his eyes as he thought about Jill and Sophie and all the things he would get to experience with Sophie that Jill would never know. He started to set the bear back on the shelf, but he couldn't quite let go of it. Telling himself he was being a sentimental fool, he carried the stuffed toy to his bed, holding it tightly as he sat down and tried once again to process everything that had happened in the past three days. He wouldn't be able to settle his grief entirely, but he also suspected that tonight would be his last moment of peace and quiet for some time to come. He'd watched the nurses at the hospital that morning. They never sat down because one of the babies always needed something: a bottle, a clean diaper, a fresh blanket. Granted, they were taking care of more than one child at a time, but they actually knew what they were doing. Srikkanth didn't have the slightest idea.

Settling on the bed, he stared at the ceiling, the bear clutched in his arms. He wanted to rail against the heavens for depriving him of his best friend and taking Sophie's mother from her before Jill even had a chance to hold the baby she had dreamed about for so long. Silently, he promised himself a day would never go by without him telling Sophie how much her mother loved her and wanted her. He would hold her and rock her and love her and give her enough affection for two parents, even if he was only one man. His daughter would grow up so loved that she wouldn't feel the lack of a mother.

THE next morning, Srikkanth was at the hospital as soon as visiting hours began. The same nurse from the day before was there. She smiled and pointed to the rocking chair and brought Sophie to him. "She had a bit of a restless night," the nurse explained. "I think she missed you."

Srikkanth shook his head in automatic denial. "She doesn't even know me. How could she possibly miss me?"

"You spent hours holding her yesterday," the nurse reminded him. "She's only three days old. She knows you better than anyone else in the world right now."

Srikkanth couldn't decide if that was more reassuring or frightening, but he could see the logic in the comment. "I don't know what I'm doing," he admitted to the nurse.

"Most first time parents don't," the woman said with an indulgent smile. "They get help from family and friends with more experience, and they make mistakes, and life goes on."

"I just don't want to do anything that might hurt her," Srikkanth explained. "My parents are in India, and I share a condo with two other bachelors. Two other gay bachelors. What do any of us know about kids?"

If the nurse was surprised by Srikkanth's revelation, she hid it well, straightening the blanket around Sophie's chest with careful hands. "Stay here with her today," she suggested. "I'll teach you what I can while I'm on shift. I get off at two, and we'll finish going over things then, when I can give you my undivided attention."

"Thank you," he said, unable to put his gratitude more clearly into words. Falling back on his childhood training, he brought his hands together, palms flat against each other as much as he was able with Sophie in his arms, bowing his head formally.

"You're welcome," the nurse said, clearly touched by the gesture. "She ate about an hour ago. I'm going to let you tell me when you think she's ready to eat again. She hasn't been a fussy baby, but she starts to get fidgety when she's hungry."

"I'll watch for it," Srikkanth promised, looking down at her peaceful face. It ought to be easy, as still as she was, to figure out when she was hungry.

He watched the nurses as they bustled around the nursery, trying to separate what was routine for all babies—and therefore something he would need to know how to do—from what was only for the sicker babies—and therefore something he wouldn't need to worry about. He watched them take temperatures and change diapers, test reflexes and feed bottles. When a sudden, foul smell emanated from the baby in his arms, he got his lesson in diapering.

The nurse laughed at the look of disgust on his face as he took off the dirty diaper and wiped Sophie clean. Srikkanth wanted to be disgruntled about the entire process, but it was hard when, redressed in a clean diaper, Sophie sighed in contentment and turned her head against his chest as if reassuring herself he was still there.

"You can say whatever you want," the nurse said with a smile. "She's your daughter now. I've been in this nursery for twenty years, and I can always tell when they figure out who their parents are."

"Really?" Srikkanth asked, feeling ridiculous for needing the reassurance.

The nurse smiled and nodded. "It's as clear as day to me," she promised. "Give me another hour and I'll go over everything with you so you can take her home."

Srikkanth smiled down at Sophie. "Are you ready for that, *betti*? Jaime and I set everything up for you last night. Your bed, your tub, your toys. All that's missing is you."

As predicted, about an hour after Srikkanth arrived, Sophie started squirming in his arms. "I think she's hungry," he called to the nurse.

"There's a pre-mixed bottle in the cabinet beneath the sink," she replied. "Open it and put it in the crock pot for about three minutes. That will warm it up for her. At home, you'll want to use a bottle warmer so you don't have to keep a crock pot hot all day."

"We bought one yesterday, but I still don't understand why I can't just use the microwave," Srikkanth said, placing Sophie carefully in her bed so he could prepare the bottle as directed.

"Don't do that!" the nurse exclaimed. "For one thing, the water doesn't always heat evenly and you could burn her mouth with it, but even more than that, the radiation can break down the proteins and keep her from getting all the nutrition she needs."

Srikkanth made a mental note to thank Jaime for making him buy a bottle warmer as he waited impatiently for the crock pot to heat the milk. He also noticed the brand name of the formula: Enfamil, as Tricia had guessed it would be. He didn't want to stop on the way home with Sophie in tow, but he was sure Jaime would either make a grocery run for him or watch Sophie while he went out later.

Srikkanth was pleased with himself when he remembered to burp Sophie part way through her meal. She smacked her lips comically when she was done before settling back into Srikkanth's arms like she didn't ever intend to move.

When the nurse finished her shift, Srikkanth had finally stopped feeling like he was going to drop her every time she moved. "You seem more at ease," she observed, sitting down beside him.

"It's starting to feel more natural," he agreed, "although I'm sure I still have a lot to learn."

"There's always more to learn," she laughed, "but most of that comes best through experience. We've talked about feeding her already, and you've changed her diaper a few times, so you can handle that. Since you're bottle-feeding her, she won't have the skin-to-skin contact that nursing babies get with their mothers. You'll want to think about that sometimes. It does a lot to soothe them. Beyond that, the biggest thing to watch no matter what you're doing is to make sure you support her head. If the bath water is a little warm or a little cool, she might be uncomfortable, but it won't hurt her in the long run. Damage to her neck could kill her if it's severe enough."

Srikkanth flinched, pulling her closer to him protectively. "What about her baths?" he asked since the nurse had brought it up.

"Every few days," the nurse advised, "or if she gets particularly dirty. The most important thing will be to keep her hands and her bottom clean. It won't be long before she starts putting her hands in her mouth, and you don't want her to get a diaper rash, because it hurts and will make her fussy."

"So how do I avoid it?" Srikkanth asked.

"Change her diaper often, especially if she's dirty, and use a protective cream; Desitin or Aquafor or Dr. Smith's all work well," the nurse advised. "You'll want to find a good pediatrician too. She'll need her vaccines and regular well-child visits."

Srikkanth's worry must have shown on his face, because the nurse patted his hand comfortingly and added, "I'll give you a list of a few the hospital works with. You can see if any of them are in your area. You'll want to get her in for a visit within a couple of weeks. She hasn't shown signs of any problems from the delivery, but it's better to have her regular doctor see her as soon as possible so he or she can get a baseline. Now is there anything else worrying you?"

"It's awfully cold outside," Srikkanth observed. "I don't want her to get sick."

"Put one more layer on her than you're wearing," the nurse suggested. "And that includes the blanket over her. You don't want her to get overheated either. So if you're wearing a shirt and a sweater, she should have a shirt, a sweater, and her blanket, or a onesie, a turtleneck, and a sweater."

"I mostly just bought sleepers for her," Srikkanth admitted, starting to worry again.

"That's fine," the nurse assured him immediately. "If you need two layers, just put two blankets over her sleeper so she'll have three layers. Or turn the heat up in the house a little so you're comfortable in just one layer of clothes."

"How soon can I take her out?" Srikkanth asked, not wanting to impose on Jaime every time he had an errand to run or needed more diapers or formula or other things for her.

"The doctors usually recommend six weeks," the nurse told him, "but I don't know that anyone actually waits that long. Obviously the more people she's around, the more she'll be exposed to germs, so keep that in mind when you're trying to decide if you should take her somewhere. Once she's had her first round of vaccines, she'll be a little safer in that respect. If people come to visit, make sure they wash their hands well before they pick her up, and if they're sick, don't let them hold her at all."

Srikkanth nodded, not mentioning that with his parents back in India, there was no one to come visit them. He had plenty of friends, but most of them wouldn't care about a new baby, and given the circumstances, his colleagues didn't even know about her yet. "Then I guess I'm ready to take her home."

"Make a well-child appointment with a doctor as soon as you can," the nurse reminded him. "That relationship will be invaluable when you have questions."

"Thank you," Srikkanth said, standing up awkwardly as he juggled the still-unfamiliar bundle in his arms. "For everything."

"You're welcome," the nurse smiled. "One of the joys of my job is seeing healthy babies go home with loving parents. You'll be fine. What she needs more than anything else is your love and attention. Give her that, and everything else will fall in line."

Looking down at Sophie's sleeping face, Srikkanth didn't think he'd have any trouble doing that.

CHAPTER FIVE

PARKING his car in the driveway outside the condo, Srikkanth took a deep breath before climbing out and opening the back door. He checked to make sure Sophie was tucked in well beneath her blanket before lifting the carrier from its base and carrying her inside. No one else was home yet, so he took her upstairs, setting the car seat down and beginning the arduous process of getting her out. She squirmed a little as he released the webbing and fumbled with supporting her head. He told himself repeatedly that it would get easier with practice and that she would learn to hold her head up on her own soon, but he still worried about hurting her. When she settled in his arms and her eyelids did not even flutter, he decided he hadn't bothered her too much.

His stomach growled hungrily, interrupting his thoughts. He debated for a moment whether he should try to take her with him while he made lunch, but he wasn't quite sure how to manage her and his food, and he had the bassinet right there. Setting her in it carefully, he tucked a light blanket around her and slipped out of the room to get some lunch. He managed to stay downstairs long enough to heat up a frozen dinner, but he'd only eaten about half of it when the need to check on Sophie grew overwhelming. He carried his plate upstairs, balancing it on his knees as he ate, his eyes glued to Sophie the entire time. It didn't matter in the least that she didn't so much as stir. He needed to see her.

He finished eating and simply stayed where he was, the plate forgotten, as he watched her sleep, until he dozed as well, the dish clattering to the floor. The noise startled them both awake, Sophie letting out an unhappy wail at being torn from her restful sleep. Srikkanth jumped up to soothe her, and she calmed somewhat when she was in his arms again, but she stayed fussier than usual. Glancing at the clock, Srikkanth saw it was almost time for her to eat anyway, so he grabbed one of the bottles of premixed formula the hospital had given him and took it downstairs along with her to heat up her snack. She fussed impatiently as they waited for the bottle warmer to do its job. He reminded himself to send Jaime a text asking him to pick up formula, but he'd have to wait until he finished feeding Sophie, because he didn't have a free hand to reach for his phone.

Once the bottle was in her mouth, she settled down, content to suck on the nipple and fill her little tummy. Srikkanth breathed a sigh of relief, still nervous about his ability to take care of her in the long run. *One day at a time,* he reminded himself. *Just take it one day at a time.*

He was so caught up in his worrying that he forgot to burp her until she had already finished the bottle. Apologizing profusely, he lifted her to his shoulder, patting her back to get the bubbles out. She let out a huge belch, followed by a gush of hot milk, all down his back.

"Forget to burp her?" Nathaniel asked, walking in the door at exactly that moment. "You really should be careful about that. It isn't good for their digestive tracts to spit up too much."

Guilt assailed Srikkanth immediately as he imagined having to explain to his pediatrician why he'd let Sophie spit up. His stomach churned, but Sophie seemed oblivious, her head resting contentedly on his shoulder.

"Here, give her to me for a minute while you change your shirt," Nathaniel said impatiently. "You stink."

Srikkanth handed Sophie to his roommate, surprised when she suddenly started crying. "Go on," Nathaniel urged. "I can hold a screaming baby for the time it takes you to change clothes. Just hurry up. I need to study."

That pretty much summed up Nathaniel's life as far as Srikkanth was concerned. Still, the man hadn't been obliged to offer, and Srikkanth really did need to change his shirt. It was cold and sticky, and Nathaniel was right about the smell. He stripped off the soiled garment, tossing it vaguely in the direction of the hamper, and pulled out a long-sleeved T-shirt this time, figuring it would be easier to get clean if Sophie spit up again and not as much of a loss if it didn't come clean. He couldn't afford to have her ruin all his work shirts.

Hurrying back downstairs, Srikkanth all but snatched Sophie from Nathaniel's arms when he saw the casual way the other man was holding her despite her continued fussiness. She blinked a couple of times when he rocked her and cooed to her and then settled down again, easing some of Srikkanth's worries. He might not have any real idea what to do with her, but at least she liked him.

Nathaniel accepted his thanks with an absent nod, disappearing into his room to study. Srikkanth looked down at Sophie. "So what am I supposed to do with you while I make dinner?" he mused. "Jaime isn't home to watch you yet, and I can hardly just put you on the floor."

Saying Jaime's name reminded him of the text he wanted to send, so he dug his phone out of his pocket and sent that off before returning to the problem of what to do with Sophie while he cooked. Maybe he should've gotten a reclining high chair for her after all. He supposed he could use her car seat. It wasn't as stable on the ground as when it was attached to the base in his car, but she wasn't moving around much, certainly not enough to squirm out of it, and if he put the straps on, she would be fine while he cooked.

He hoped.

Usually Srikkanth enjoyed cooking, but this time he was distracted, feeling the need to glance in Sophie's direction every few seconds to make sure she was safe and happy in her car seat serving an unintended purpose. He only hoped dinner was edible, since he'd overcooked the onions and nearly burnt the spice mixture he used in his mother's chicken curry.

JAIME smiled as he looked at the text on his phone. Srikkanth had obviously gotten home with Sophie if he was already sending messages asking for help. Jaime had a break he hadn't used today since the store had been so busy he'd needed everyone on the floor. Not that he was complaining, but he couldn't skimp on his employees' breaks, which meant he'd skimped on his. Glancing at the clock, he decided that he'd just take his lunch and his break now and leave forty-five minutes early. He had two assistant managers already on the floor, and they could page him if they needed him. Flipping open his phone, he dialed Srikkanth's number and waited for him to answer.

"Hello?"

Srikkanth's voice was so distracted that Jaime smiled again. "I didn't wake Sophie, did I?" he asked.

"No," Srikkanth replied. "She's sleeping in her car seat while I try to cook dinner."

"Good. Do you have a minute, or am I going to ruin dinner by distracting you?"

Srikkanth snorted. "We'll be lucky if dinner's edible at all tonight. I can't seem to concentrate on anything but her."

Jaime laughed. Srikkanth sounded adorably ruffled, so unlike his usually composed self. "I think that's probably pretty normal," he assured his friend. "I'm leaving work now, so I'll stop at the store and pick up the things you texted me about. Do you need anything else?"

"I think we got everything we needed for her yesterday except the formula," Srikkanth replied.

"I didn't ask if she needed anything," Jaime reminded him. "I asked if you needed anything."

"A bottle of vodka?" Srikkanth quipped. "A hole in the head?"

Jaime chuckled. "Stop worrying so much and enjoy having her. Tell me what she looks like."

As he waited for Srikkanth to answer, he pulled on his coat and waved good-bye to his assistant manager. The woman waved back, and Jaime put work behind him for the day.

"She looks like Jill," Srikkanth replied immediately.

"She can't possibly look like Jill," Jaime retorted, thinking of the fair-skinned, red-haired woman he'd seen at Srikkanth's side any number of times. "You're too dark for her to have Jill's coloring."

"She has my coloring," Srikkanth agreed. Jaime fumbled for his keys in his pocket, trying not to drop the phone at the same time. "Dark hair, dark eyes, although her skin isn't as dark as mine, at least not right now."

"Well, she is a mixture of both of you," Jaime mused as he climbed in the car and pulled out of the parking lot, "so it makes sense she'd be a little lighter than you are. She might get darker as she gets a little older too. I remember my mama saying that babies' pigmentation sometimes didn't show up fully for a couple of months."

"Other than her coloring, though, she looks like Jill," Srikkanth continued, his voice tender. "She's got the same eyes and mouth, and I think her hair will be curly too."

"I'm sure she'll be as beautiful as her mother," Jaime said, thinking quietly that she could do far worse than looking like her father. He'd noticed Srikkanth as soon as he answered the ad looking for a roommate, but they'd agreed up front that good roommates were even harder to find than a good lay and that as long as they were roommates, they wouldn't get involved in other ways. It had worked out great. They'd had boyfriends come and go over the three years they'd shared the condo, and even a couple of third roommates, but their friendship had remained solid. He figured that was a pretty good track record, although he couldn't help but wonder how Sophie would change things.

"I hope so," Srikkanth murmured, "although that could make high school interesting."

"Don't borrow trouble," Jaime advised. "You've got a few years before you have to worry about that. Let's get her into kindergarten before you start thinking about high school, okay?"

"Damn it!"

"What's wrong?" Jaime asked immediately, hoping nothing had happened to Sophie.

Srikkanth sighed. "I ruined dinner."

Jaime smiled. "Don't worry about it. I'll stop and get Chinese on the way home. I'm at the store now, so I'll get the formula. Call and place an order. I'll pick it up when I go by."

Srikkanth sighed again. "Okay, let me go see what Nathaniel wants. What about you? You want chicken with cashews as usual?"

"That's fine," Jaime said, amused at how well they knew each other after three years.

"Okay, I'll call it in. Keep the receipt so I can pay you back when you get home," Srikkanth said.

Jaime started to protest, but Srikkanth had already hung up. "Watch it, Bhattacharya," Jaime muttered at the phone as he parked and went into the store. "You're going to start letting me help you if I have to tie you down and make you."

He grabbed the formula Srikkanth had named in his message, not really knowing how much to get. His mother had nursed his siblings, so this was one thing he didn't have a lot of experience with. He could change diapers in his sleep, but he'd have to learn about bottles along with Srikkanth. He didn't mind.

The cashier at the hole-in-the-wall Chinese restaurant recognized him and handed him his order almost before he'd had a chance to say hello. Jaime paid and thanked the woman as always, but instead of lingering and chatting like he usually did, he headed back to his car and drove the rest of the way back to their complex without delay. Their condo was one of about thirty in the complex, all of them less than ten years old. All virtually identical. It was a far cry from the old house he'd grown up in, his parents having bought it for next to nothing because it was in such terrible shape. They'd spent years fixing it up, always some project going on. It had been a wonderful way to grow up, the family all pitching in to patch this wall or paint that room until his parents had one of the nicest houses in the neighborhood. Jaime didn't have a family, though, a group of people to come home to and build with, so the condo was a compromise. It wasn't even his, really, since he rented from Srikkanth, but he didn't need more than he had at the moment, and it let him save the bulk of his income towards retirement and a down payment on something of his own at a later date. He'd entertained the notion on occasion of finding someone to share those dreams with, but so far he hadn't met anyone he felt that strongly about. Certainly not strongly enough to give up his current situation, which was pretty much ideal as far as he could tell, other than the absence of a long-term partner in his life. He wasn't quite ready to give up on Randy, his current boyfriend, but Randy hadn't given any indication of being interested in more than having a good time.

Juggling bags to carry everything inside in one trip, Jaime tapped softly at the door rather than ringing the bell. He vividly remembered his mother demanding his father disable their doorbell at one point when it seemed like every time she got his fractious sister to sleep, someone would ring the bell. Fortunately, Srikkanth heard him, arriving seconds later to let him inside.

"Thank you," Srikkanth said before Jaime had even gotten in the door. "Nathaniel came out of his room demanding to know what the awful smell was after I burned dinner. I told him you were bringing Chinese, but I don't think he was terribly impressed."

"Don't worry about him," Jaime soothed immediately, handing Srikkanth the bag with the formula. "I swear he complains just to have something to talk about. He'll get over it once he's had something to eat."

"I hope you're right."

"Come on, don't worry about him. I want to see Sophie," Jaime insisted, changing the subject away from their sometimes-difficult roommate.

"She's in the kitchen sleeping," Srikkanth replied, leading the way through the living room to the kitchen where Sophie lay, as promised, asleep in her car seat.

"You know," Jaime teased, "you could've put her either in her stroller, since it has a reclining seat, or in the napper from her playpen. It detaches, remember?"

"As much trouble as we had getting it put together in the first place, I think I'll leave it where it is," Srikkanth said with a short laugh. "She was fine in her car seat."

Jaime let it go at that, but he remembered some of the seats he'd seen at Babies Я Us, the ones with lights and music that would probably annoy Nathaniel to no end, but they'd amuse Sophie, which was far more important than Nathaniel's attitude. Maybe he'd see about getting one for her later in the week. In the meantime, he'd see how else he could spoil her rotten. She stirred about that time. "Get the bottle together," he told Srikkanth. "I'll see if I can distract her until it's ready."

"Maybe I should hold her," Srikkanth began. "She didn't react very well when I handed her to Nathaniel."

Jaime ignored him, lifting Sophie deftly out of her seat and cradling her with the ease of much familiarity. Yes, it had been a few years, but he hadn't forgotten how to hold a baby. Holding a baby, like riding a bike, simply wasn't something one forgot how to do. Her eyes opened as she stared up at him, but he rocked her and cooed at her while Srikkanth fumbled with the can of formula. He could tell she was a little confused at having someone else holding her, but he just kept rocking and talking, and she calmed in his arms while they waited for Srikkanth to get the bottle heated up. "Hello, precious," he murmured. "Were you a good girl for your father today? We're very glad you're here, he and I, even if Nathaniel is an old sourpuss who can't appreciate a good thing when he sees it."

The bottle warmer did as it promised, heating the bottle evenly and rapidly. Jaime was tempted to ask if he could feed her, but he figured it was too early for that, so he passed her back to her father and watched with a smile as she fed eagerly.

"Is the food here yet?" Nathaniel's voice interrupted the moment of peace.

"It's on the table," Jaime said softly, his eyes not leaving Srikkanth and Sophie. "You can take it into your room so we don't keep you from your studies."

Nathaniel scowled as he dug in the sack and pulled out his meal, but he didn't say anything else, disappearing back into his room as Srikkanth burped Sophie before giving her the rest of her meal.

"I don't think he likes her," Srikkanth commented softly when Nathaniel's bedroom door shut again.

"I don't think he likes much of anything that might keep him from studying," Jaime joked. "He's always glaring at me if I have company over."

"It's been too long since I last had anyone I wanted to have over," Srikkanth replied. "I guess I haven't had the pleasure of him scowling at me for that reason, but he pays his rent on time, helps around the place, and isn't a slob. I'd say we're still coming out ahead."

"Oh, definitely," Jaime agreed, thinking about Nathaniel's predecessor, who'd left dirty dishes and dirty laundry and a few less pleasant things strewn all over the common areas of the condo. "Here, give her to me for a bit so you can eat your dinner before it gets cold."

"What about your dinner?" Srikkanth asked.

"I perfected the art of eating one-handed a long time ago," Jaime replied, reaching for Sophie. "Now, are you going to share?"

Srikkanth hesitated for a moment before agreeing. "I suppose it's all right. She didn't seem to mind you holding her a bit ago. She screamed her head off when I gave her to Nathaniel."

Jaime settled Sophie in the crook of his arm. "And why would you do that?"

"Because she'd spit up all over my shirt," Srikkanth explained, pulling containers out of the bag and setting them out on the table. "He offered to hold her while I changed clothes."

"That was nice of him," Jaime agreed. "So she didn't care for that?"

"Not at all."

"Well, I'm glad she likes me," Jaime said, leaning down and kissing her forehead softly, feeling his heart swell in his chest.

CHAPTER SIX

SRIKKANTH was at his wits' end. After dinner, he'd taken Sophie back upstairs to sleep. She'd snuggled into her napper and gone straight to sleep. Now, an hour later, she was screaming for no reason Srikkanth could figure out. She refused a bottle; her diaper was clean; he'd checked to make sure her clothes weren't pinching her anywhere. He'd walked with her, sung to her, rocked her as much as he could—everything he could think of, and still she screamed. So he started over, with no success. When he was just about ready to admit defeat, Jaime appeared in his doorway.

"Give her to me," Jaime said. "Go for a run or something to get a break."

"But—"

"My sister had colic, and when she got like this, all we could do was take turns so no one threw her against the wall," Jaime insisted. "She's going to keep screaming whether you're here or not. Take a break and you can try again to calm her down when you get back."

Srikkanth hesitated a moment longer, but his frustration level was getting high. A short run would do him good, restoring his patience if nothing else. He hoped so, anyway. With a sigh and a kiss on Sophie's forehead, he passed her to Jaime, only to have her screams redouble in volume. He made to take her back, but Jaime shook his head. "I'll be fine for fifteen or twenty minutes. Go for a short run."

Quickly, before Jaime had time to change his mind, Srikkanth pulled on his running gear and headed downstairs. Nathaniel intercepted him before he reached the door.

"I told you this was a bad idea," he snapped. "How am I supposed to study if she's screaming like that?"

"I don't know," Srikkanth said, running out the door before his roommate could say anything else. He wanted to believe Jaime and trust that loving Sophie would be enough to make up for all his ignorance and inexperience, but Nathaniel's negativity was more immediate, more real. Far easier to accept. He obviously couldn't take care of Sophie, or she wouldn't be upstairs screaming her head off. She was a baby. She wasn't old enough to scream just to be difficult. If she was that upset, something was wrong. His feet hit the pavement in a steady rhythm as he tried to clear his thoughts and forget everything but the exhilaration of his run. His thoughts weren't as easily left behind as the sound of Sophie's screaming.

The nurse at the hospital said she was a happy baby, but her first night home with him, she was already inconsolable. He didn't think he'd done anything to upset her, but he didn't really have any way to know other than to compare the way she was acting now with the way she'd acted at the hospital. He certainly hadn't seen her fuss like this at the hospital. Maybe she missed the nurses? She'd been with them far more than she'd been with him.

He couldn't take her back to the hospital, though. He'd committed to rearing her, and now he had to follow through. He just wished he knew how. He supposed he could call his mother, but that would mean explaining the situation, why he hadn't told them about the baby sooner, and all the rest. He'd have to tell them eventually because he couldn't very well keep his daughter secret from her grandparents all her life, but he needed a few days to get used to the idea of being a father before he tried to explain everything to his parents.

Feeling guilty for leaving Jaime with his problem, Srikkanth cut short his usual circuit, simply circling the condo complex instead of taking his usual route around the neighborhood. When he arrived back at home, he paused for a moment on the doorstep, steeling his nerves to return to Sophie's screaming. Opening the door, however, he heard only silence.

He frowned as he climbed the steps, wondering where Jaime had taken Sophie. When he reached his bedroom, though, Jaime sat on the bed, Sophie cradled in his arms. He lifted a finger to his lips and gestured for Srikkanth to go back downstairs. Standing carefully, he set Sophie gently in her napper and slipped from the room, shutting the door behind him.

"She fell asleep about five minutes after you left," Jaime whispered. "I think she was exhausted."

"Or she likes you better," Srikkanth said bitterly.

Jaime shook his head immediately. "Don't even think that," he insisted, leading Srikkanth into his room next door so they could talk without disturbing Sophie. "Babies get colic. Some of them get it worse than others, but it happens. There isn't anything you can do about it except what we did: hold her 'til she wears herself out and falls asleep. It doesn't make it any easier to listen to her scream, but you didn't do anything wrong. I promise."

"I just feel so helpless," Srikkanth complained, knowing it made him sound whiny but beyond caring. "She wasn't like this at the hospital. The nurses said she was a quiet baby, not fussy at all."

"Sri, she's three days old," Jaime reminded him. "She's not old enough to make that kind of generalizations about. And even if she were, babies' personalities change as they develop just like other people's do. Her first night home is probably a part of it, yes, but that doesn't mean you did anything wrong. No matter what you'd decided for her, she'd have left the hospital eventually, which means she'd have to deal with a new environment. You made the right choice. It won't always be easy, but you'll make it work."

"You're so sure of it," Srikkanth marveled.

Jaime shrugged, not sure how to put into words what he was feeling. "Babies belong with their parents," he said after a moment.

"I know adoption works, and I certainly don't want kids growing up in abusive or neglectful situations, but this isn't like that. You have the means to take care of her, and I can tell you already love her. Next to that, everything else is a technicality. All parents make mistakes, especially with the first baby, because they don't know what they're doing. Most of them are pure ignorance and nothing to really worry about."

"And the ones that aren't?" Srikkanth demanded.

Jaime shrugged. "The ones that are more serious are almost always negligent if not worse. You may be more inexperienced than most, but you don't have it in you to be negligent. If you're really worried about something, ask me. If I don't know, I'll call my mama. She knows everything, and she's closer than your mother."

"Does she have a cure for colic?" Srikkanth asked with a soft laugh. "Since I failed spectacularly with that one today."

"I don't know if she does or not. Let's see what we can look up and if we don't find anything, I'll call her," Jaime proposed.

Srikkanth nodded. It hadn't even occurred to him to search online because he hadn't known what was wrong, but now that he had a name for the problem, he could figure out what to do for it. His computer was in his room, though, and he didn't want to risk Sophie waking up before he knew what to do for her. "Can I use your computer?"

"Of course," Jaime exclaimed. "Come on. Let's see what we can find."

They flipped open Jaime's laptop and started searching. An hour later, they had a list of options to try, ranging from swaddling and cuddling with her to startling her out of her crying with the vacuum cleaner to taking her for a walk to get a change of scenery. About the time they finished searching, Sophie woke up. Srikkanth steeled himself for another fit like before, but she settled down as soon as he gave her a bottle. When she was done, she smuggled into his arms, watching him owlishly. Srikkanth rolled his eyes at Jaime. "What's this?" he joked.

"She was testing you," Jaime grinned. "She wanted to see if you could figure out what to do with her."

"I think we all could've done without that," Srikkanth said drolly. "Nathaniel in particular."

"Did he say something?" Jaime asked sharply.

"Yeah, he snarled at me as I was leaving."

"I know what you can do about Nathaniel," Jaime said with a moue of disgust. "Ignore him. You already know what he's like, and if you weren't upset about Sophie, you wouldn't have given his comment a second thought."

"I know," Srikkanth replied, "but I was upset about Sophie, and he does live here. We knew when he moved in that he wanted a quiet place to live. That's why you moved up here—so he could have the downstairs bedroom and be away from more of the noise."

"Whose name is on the deed?" Jaime demanded. "Yours, not his. He can deal with it or find another place to live."

It wasn't quite that simple. Srikkanth depended on the rent from his housemates to pay the mortgage on the condo, especially now that he was going to have the extra expense of a baby. He'd have to look for a smaller place if Nathaniel and Jaime moved out. He wasn't going to worry about that tonight, though. He had enough to worry about with Sophie and getting through the night.

THE days fell into a routine for Srikkanth, sleeping when Sophie slept, feeding her every two hours, grabbing a bite to eat when he could. Somewhat to his surprise, he found that he didn't miss work at all, his fascination with Sophie sufficient to fill his days. The suggestions for dealing with colic seemed to work far better during the day than at night. Jaime continued to be Srikkanth's rock, taking Sophie for half an hour or more each night so Srikkanth could get in a run.

For his part, Jaime enjoyed the time he spent with Sophie, even beginning to seek excuses to spend more time with her and Srikkanth. When she wasn't colicky, she was an engaging baby, her personality becoming clearer and clearer with each passing day. He hated to hear her cry, more because he knew how much it upset Srikkanth than because it bothered him. He knew enough about babies to understand that she was uncomfortable and that it would pass, so he simply held her and rocked her or walked her around the house until she quieted down or until Srikkanth returned from his run. He'd also gotten really good at ignoring Nathaniel's glares and deflecting his comments before they could upset Srikkanth even more.

About three weeks after Sophie came home from the hospital, Jaime went upstairs as usual to take Sophie so Srikkanth could go for a run. The sight that met his eyes stole his breath and made his heart pound faster in his chest. Srikkanth sat on his bed, bare to the waist, Sophie in only her diaper cradled to his chest. Srikkanth's skin was dark against Sophie's slightly paler coloring.

"You're going to spoil her," Jaime said, trying to keep his voice steady. He'd seen Srikkanth shirtless before, but not often and always in the process of changing clothes rather than simply sitting around without a top. At the moment, though, Srikkanth didn't seem to have any intention of getting dressed, and that was doing all manner of things to Jaime's libido. He reminded himself that he had a boyfriend of sorts at the moment, but it wasn't like he was acting on the sudden attraction. There wasn't any harm in acknowledging another man's attractiveness if he didn't do anything but look, was there?

"The nurse at the hospital said I should hold her this way," Srikkanth replied calmly. "She said bottle-fed babies don't get skin-to-skin contact while they're nursing, so they need it at other times to help with bonding." He sent Jaime a beatific smile that went straight to Jaime's cock. "I don't know if it's doing her any good, but it certainly feels good to me. She's so soft and smooth."

Staring at Srikkanth's chest, Jaime thought Sophie wasn't the only one who was smooth.

The doorbell rang, followed swiftly by Nathaniel yelling for Jaime. "Your date's here."

"Shit," Jaime muttered, forgetting for a moment that Sophie was in the room. "Shoot, sorry, Sri. I'll have to get used to watching my mouth again. I forgot I was supposed to go out with Randy tonight. I can see if he'd mind waiting so you can still get in your run."

"Don't worry about it," Srikkanth replied, leaning down and kissing Sophie's cheek. "We'll be fine for tonight. Go enjoy your date. We'll be here when you get home."

Jaime nodded, backing out of the room slowly, wishing he didn't have to leave. When they'd made the date, Sophie hadn't been in the picture and he'd been looking forward to seeing Beecake at a local pub, but now, he wanted nothing more than to stay home and spend his uninterrupted hour with Sophie. There was nothing to be done for it. Randy was here, and they'd already paid for the tickets and made dinner reservations at the club. He'd just have to cajole Srikkanth into letting him spend a little extra time with her over the next few days. It was Friday. Maybe he could even steal her for a few hours tomorrow, since he didn't have to work.

"I'll just be a few minutes," he called down to Randy. "I'm not quite ready."

He changed clothes quickly into something more appropriate for a night out than the jeans and sweatshirt he was currently wearing, thinking the entire time how much more comfortable he'd be if he could just stay home. Before he went down the stairs to join Randy, he peeked in Srikkanth's room again to get one more glimpse of him and Sophie together to hold him through the evening. If that wasn't a sad state of affairs, he didn't know what was.

As he suspected, Randy was sitting impatiently on the couch in the living room waiting for him. "What took you so long?" he snapped.

"I was helping Srikkanth with something," Jaime replied, not really wanting to get into an explanation of Sophie and everything else. She was too special to share, and somehow he doubted Randy would get it any more than Nathaniel did.

Randy huffed in annoyance, but Jaime ignored him. He'd been looking forward to the chance to see Billy Boyd and his band in concert since he'd heard they were coming to town and he refused to let his "date" ruin that, even if he'd already decided he wouldn't have time for another night out any time soon should the other man ask. Maybe—Jaime hoped it wasn't just wishful thinking—Randy would be annoyed enough with his tardiness and general uncommunicativeness to refrain from trying to set another date. If not, Jaime had the perfect excuse. He'd simply tell Randy he had to babysit for Sophie.

WHEN the concert ended four hours later, Jaime had to admit he was glad he'd gone. The pub had delivered on its promise of an intimate setting, only seating about one hundred fifty people total, and the table he and Randy had reserved ended up being about ten feet from the stage. While they were waiting to get in, Billy Boyd had come out front to sign autographs and shoot the breeze with his fans. Once they'd gotten inside and the band came out, the evening had only gotten better. Billy chatted to the crowd like they were close personal friends, even exchanging quips with a group of women a few tables back that had Jaime doubled over laughing. The music had been spectacular, and Jaime had enjoyed every minute of the show.

If only he'd enjoyed the rest of the evening as much. Randy had been pretty much obnoxious except when the band was playing. Jaime wasn't sure if he'd never noticed before or if his date was worse tonight than before. He knew he was less patient than usual with anything that kept him from home. For the past couple of weeks, he'd caught himself watching the clock at work, feeling the last hour drag like two, his thoughts fixed on Sophie and getting home to see her as quickly as possible. Tonight was no different, the thought of her going to bed without his giving her a good-night kiss almost enough to make him reject Randy's invitation to linger for another round of drinks after the show ended. A quick glance at his watch showed the time already too late for Sophie's regular bedtime, but she would be awake again during the night for a bottle. If Srikkanth was still awake when he got home, he'd offer to get up with her once, and if he wasn't, Jaime could still sneak in for a kiss when he heard her wake up.

As Randy went to the bar to get their drinks, Jaime's thoughts drifted back to Srikkanth holding Sophie before he left. He couldn't help thinking how much Srikkanth would have enjoyed the concert and probably the break, although Sophie had been easier to deal with the last few days. Maybe he could offer to babysit for longer than just a run so Sri could go out for a movie or on a date. Even as he thought it, he knew he didn't want that, a rather hypocritical thought given where he was at the moment. There was their agreement not to get involved with each other to consider, but a lot of things had changed in the past few weeks. He ignored Randy's hints that they should go back to his place and resisted the other man's blandishments urging him to agree to another date. Jaime wasn't sure why Randy was trying so hard. It wasn't like he was putting out or had any intention of doing so any time soon. When Randy persisted, Jaime finally snapped. "Look, we've had some fun together, but that's all it is. Things have changed, and I won't have nearly as much free time from here on."

"We could still spend the time you do have together," Randy said hopefully.

Jaime shook his head. "Thanks, but no."

That was the end of easy conversation and sharing drinks. Jaime paid his portion of the tab and insisted he could take a taxi home. He just wanted to get away from Randy and back home with Sophie and Srikkanth where he belonged.

CHAPTER SEVEN

"I WAS thinking about getting a rocking chair," Srikkanth told Jaime as he was making dinner a few days later. Sophie was awake, and Jaime had offered to hold her while Srikkanth cooked. Sophie didn't seem to have any complaints about it, sitting happily in Jaime's lap while Srikkanth puttered around the kitchen. They'd fallen into a routine even before Jaime's date, but since that night when Jaime came into his room while he was giving Sophie a bottle to kiss her goodnight, Jaime had hardly left Sophie's side except to work and sleep. Sophie had started to recognize Jaime, too, reaching for him the same way she reached for Srikkanth. Srikkanth had vacillated between jealousy and relief for as long as it took him to remember that most babies grew up with—loved—two parents without their affection for one in any way diminishing their affection for the other. Once he'd given himself that kick in the pants, he'd stopped worrying about accepting Jaime's offers of assistance. Besides, he didn't know how he'd manage without Jaime's help.

"That's a good idea," Jaime agreed. "I don't know that it'll fit in your room, though."

"Yeah, I'd have to put it downstairs in the living room, but that puts it—and us—out in Nathaniel's way even more than we already are."

"You already know my opinion on that matter," Jaime said, his lip curling at the thought of the ever more negative comments their third roommate had made over the past few weeks. "Sophie's here to stay, so he can either get over it or move somewhere else."

Srikkanth couldn't argue with that except that it left him in a bind as far as the mortgage was concerned. He'd have to find another renter, and that would be even more difficult now that they'd have to tell any new housemate that there was a baby in the house along with two gay men. He couldn't afford to force the issue.

"How long until dinner?" Nathaniel called from his room.

"About twenty minutes," Srikkanth called back, checking the timer on the rice.

Nathaniel didn't reply, but a moment later they heard the water running in the shower. Jaime rolled his eyes and refrained from mentioning *again* how much Nathaniel was getting on his nerves. Srikkanth knew already, and complaining didn't do anything but spread negativity. His mother had lectured him repeatedly when he was younger about having a positive attitude and not adding negative energy to the world. "If you can't say anything nice, don't say anything at all" was still her favorite adage. He wasn't completely convinced she was right, but he'd learned the lesson anyway. He found it hard to be negative verbally in all but the most extreme circumstances.

About the time the rice was ready, Nathaniel came into the kitchen. "I'll be moving out at the end of the month," he announced. "I've found a new apartment where I'll be more assured of peace and quiet. I can't study with all the baby's noise."

Srikkanth nodded silently, knowing it had only been a matter of time. He did some quick calculating, trying to figure out how long he could afford to make up Nathaniel's portion of the mortgage before he'd be in trouble financially. He figured he could make it a couple of months before they absolutely had to have a new roommate again.

"Thanks for letting me know early in the month," he said finally. "The sooner I start looking for someone to move in, the better."

Nathaniel nodded in return, serving a plateful of rice and curry and returning to his room to study.

"Do you really want to try to break in a new housemate with Sophie already here?" Jaime asked when Nathaniel's door shut behind him.

"It doesn't matter what I want," Srikkanth replied. "I have to pay the mortgage, and I can't make up the difference for very many months without a third person chipping in."

"Can you pay half?" Jaime asked.

Srikkanth calculated quickly. "Yes, but that isn't fair to you. You moved in with the understanding that you'd pay five hundred a month in rent."

Jaime shrugged. "I can afford a bit extra, and we can use the extra room as a nursery. Sophie's going to outgrow your room before too long. That way you'll have a bit of privacy back as well."

Srikkanth shook his head and stared at Jaime in bemusement. "Why are you doing this?"

"Because no one should have to raise a baby alone," Jaime replied as if it were the most obvious answer in the world.

"I appreciate the offer," Srikkanth said slowly, "but I'd feel better if I at least look for someone to take Nathaniel's room. I'll put some ads out tomorrow and see what happens."

"Let me know if you have any interviews," Jaime requested. "I'd like to meet whoever might be moving in."

"Of course!" Srikkanth exclaimed. "It wouldn't be fair to you to have someone move in without your approval. Whatever we decide to do, we'll decide it together."

Jaime left it at that as Srikkanth dished up a plate for him and set it on the table where he could reach it. Looking down at Sophie, Jaime smiled and kissed her forehead again before picking up his fork.

As he started to eat, Jaime tried to imagine adding another person to their table. It was easy to imagine Sophie there in a few years, but the thought of sharing her attention with a third adult now did not appeal at all. He told himself that was ridiculous, but his head didn't seem to have any control over his heart in this matter. He could accept it and move on or fight it and fail. He figured he might as well accept it and figure out how to make sure he didn't end up in an untenable solution. He doubted Srikkanth would find many takers anyway, given that they'd have to share the condo with two men and a baby, but Jaime decided right then to find a reason to reject anyone who was seriously interested. Sophie needed her own space, and so did Srikkanth, and that meant keeping Nathaniel's room unoccupied.

"That's quite a scowl on your face," Srikkanth commented. "Is everything all right?"

Consciously, Jaime summoned a smile. "Yes, I was just thinking about the hassle of finding a new roommate. Are you sure that's necessary? Couldn't I just move down here so we can turn my room into a proper nursery? She can have her own bed, and you can get the rocking chair you were talking about earlier. And that way she'll have a place for her toys."

It was tempting, Srikkanth had to admit to himself, but it didn't seem fair to Jaime. He'd see how things went with the interviews and go from there.

THE smell of cigarette smoke clung to the clothes of the first person they met. Srikkanth had run out of space in the ad after mentioning two men and a baby in the condo and hadn't had room for his usual no-smoker comment. He grimaced at the stench. Even across the room, he saw Jaime's nose twitch and then Sophie's little face scrunch up as the stale odor reached them. Srikkanth went through the niceties, but they all knew this was a pointless interview. "So you're a smoker?" he asked after a few minutes.

The man shrugged. "I have one occasionally."

"With the baby in the house, we really can't have you smoking here," Srikkanth said, not needing Jaime to tell him that.

"Oh, it's not a problem," the prospective renter said with a smile. "I can always go outside. You've got a patio, right? That's fine for me."

Srikkanth wasn't sure what he thought of that, but he completed the interview anyway. The only time he'd ever accepted a roommate on the spot was Jaime, and while that had worked out incredibly well, he wanted to discuss any decisions with his friend, particularly since Jaime knew so much more about what Sophie would need than he did.

"No way," Jaime said as soon as the man closed the door on his way out. "If he smokes enough to smell that strong, he'll still expose Sophie to the toxins. Thirdhand smoke isn't quite as bad as secondhand smoke, but that doesn't mean it's good for her."

"I wasn't sure," Srikkanth agreed, "but it makes sense. I mean, it's unpleasant to be around even if it weren't harmful."

"For all of us." Jaime cradled Sophie closer protectively, glad he didn't have to persuade Srikkanth out of this one.

Srikkanth nodded. "I'll call him later and let him know to keep looking then. I've only had one other person interested. She's coming at the end of the week to meet us."

"She?" Jaime repeated, not sure how he felt about adding a woman to their comfortably masculine existence. Sophie didn't count. Not at three weeks old, for sure!

Srikkanth shrugged. "I didn't see any harm in meeting her. We've always had male roommates, but that's more a question of the way it worked out than because of anything set in stone, at least for my part."

Jaime tried to think about it objectively, but every image assailing him detailed the woman swooping in, seeing Sophie, and taking over her care, leaving Jaime, if not Srikkanth, out in the cold.

"We can meet her," he said, not able to work up any enthusiasm for the thought.

IF JAIME hadn't been looking for a reason to reject any roommate, he suspected he'd have been fine with Julie, the woman who came to interview with them on Friday. She was polite, had good references, had a steady job, and could move in immediately. The only problem was the fact that she only needed a place for six months while she was working on a project. Once that was over, she'd be moving out again. Before Sophie, that wouldn't have particularly posed a problem for Jaime and Srikkanth. It gave them time to search for a longer-term roommate, but Jaime didn't want a new roommate, short or long term. When the woman left, he turned to Srikkanth.

"I don't like the idea of someone moving in for just a couple of months," he said. "Sophie needs more stability than that. She'll get attached to Julie and then Julie will be gone and she won't understand why. If we're going to have someone move in, it needs to be someone who plans to stay."

"For how long?" Srikkanth asked worriedly. "I mean, we can't expect someone to commit to moving in here with us until Sophie's grown."

"No, of course not," Jaime agreed, "but we don't want a revolving door either. At her age, she needs to form attachments that last more than a few months. It's incredibly important for babies to have that kind of stability."

"All right," Srikkanth conceded. "I'll tell Julie we're not interested."

THEY got a call about a week later from another person interested in their ad. Jaime grimaced behind his hand when Srikkanth told him, wondering what excuse he could possibly use to reject this one. He agreed to the meeting time Srikkanth proposed and spent the week plotting ways to convince Srikkanth not to let anyone move in. Ever.

The third applicant seemed like a perfectly reasonable guy, a shift worker at Good Samaritan who currently worked nights. Jaime could tell Srikkanth was leaning toward accepting him as a renter, and again, if it had just been the two of them, Jaime probably would've agreed. He wanted the extra space for Sophie though, so after the man left, he turned to Srikkanth with a disappointed look on his face. "I know she isn't sleeping through the night at the moment," he began, "but Sophie needs to learn the difference between day and night, and having someone on an opposite schedule risks throwing that all off. You don't want her to be awake all night, especially when you have to go back to work."

Srikkanth frowned. "Are you sure? I really liked this one."

"I did too," Jaime assured him, "but we have to think about what's best for Sophie. Would you rather I call to tell him?"

In the end, Srikkanth had called, feeling it was his responsibility since he was the one who'd placed the ad. He let the ad expire at the end of the week, giving in to Jaime's insistence that they use the extra room for Sophie. They couldn't move anything in for her until Nathaniel moved out, but Jaime convinced Srikkanth to go shopping for her anyway. They could put the furniture in storage until the room was ready, he insisted.

As with everything else where Sophie was concerned, Srikkanth let himself be persuaded. They returned to Babies Я Us in search of the perfect crib set and rocking chair. The rocker was easy. Srikkanth loved the gliders, so then the only question was what color wood and fabric to get.

"Let's look at cribs and then you can see what matches," Jaime suggested. "After all, there's a lot more variety with the cribs than with the gliders."

Srikkanth agreed and let Jaime take him over to the selection of cribs and bedding sets. He grimaced at the first several they passed, all frills and lace and princesses. "You aren't going to be a prissy girl, are you?" he asked Sophie, asleep in her stroller. "I won't know what to do with you if you are."

"There are plenty of other options," Jaime reminded him. "We don't have to pick something just because she's a girl. We can pick whatever we want for her. Even if it isn't a typical thing for a girl."

"Yeah, but I don't particularly like the boats and trains and stuff for the boys either," Srikkanth said.

"They've got gender-neutral stuff too," Jaime pointed out. "Look at this one." He showed Srikkanth a comforter set with four panes of different stuffed animals snuggled together. "This one isn't girly at all."

Srikkanth looked at it for a moment, stroking the soft material of the quilt. "It looks nice," he agreed.

"And it's on sale," Jaime pointed out. "Half off, and for almost twice as many pieces as some of the other products."

"Okay, okay," Srikkanth laughed. "You've sold me. Now we just have to find a crib."

Jaime grinned and followed Srikkanth to the furniture section of the store. "Pick something you can convert and that she can use later, not just as a baby," Jaime advised. "Otherwise you'll be buying new furniture for her again in a few years."

"That makes sense," Srikkanth agreed, walking slowly through the displays. He stopped finally at one in dark cherry. Studying the long sides that would turn into the headboard and footboard of a double bed, he decided they wouldn't be out of place in a teenager's or even an adult's bedroom. "And it has a matching chest and armoire. So all we need is a cherry glider and footstool and we'll be ready."

"See," Jaime teased. "I told you Sophie needed her own room. We can still use the playpen when she's sleeping downstairs or when we want to keep her in one place while she's awake."

"If we're going to have some extra room, maybe we could look at a swing for her too," Srikkanth mused, glancing over at the display.

"We need a high chair first," Jaime disagreed. "She can sleep downstairs in the playpen, but we can't feed her there, and I'm not sure it will fit in the kitchen. We need a place for her when we're cooking."

Srikkanth chuckled. "I don't know why you'd think that. You just hold her when I'm cooking anyway. She won't need the high chair for herself until she's six months old. I think that can wait a bit longer. If you think the swing would take up too much space, we could get a little reclining chair for her, like the ones next to the swings."

"Is this your daughter?" Tricia, the woman who had helped them so much the first time they were at Babies Я Us, asked, coming up to peek into the stroller.

"Yes, this is Sophie," Srikkanth said, tipping the hood of the stroller back so Tricia could see Sophie better.

As if hearing her name, Sophie's eyes opened. She blinked a couple of times before her eyes fixed on Srikkanth.

"She's beautiful," Tricia said, smiling down at Sophie. "So did you decide you needed more stuff for her?"

"Our third roommate decided to move out, which means we have room now to set up a nursery for her," Jaime explained. "We were looking at furniture for her."

"And trying to decide between a swing and a little seat for her," Srikkanth added. "Do you have any thoughts or suggestions?"

"The bouncers are generally less expensive than the swings, they take up less space, and they tend to have more in the way of lights, music, and toys to keep the baby entertained while she's awake as well as lull her to sleep with vibrations," Tricia replied. "I've known people who have both or who really prefer the swing over the bouncer, but for the most part, the bouncers are sufficient. I had one friend whose baby needed the rocking motion to sleep, but beyond that, most people use them pretty much interchangeably."

"Even with Nathaniel moving out, space is still a consideration," Srikkanth mused aloud. "I think we'd be better off with a bouncer."

"My favorite is the aquarium one," Tricia confided. "You can turn it on and leave it on, or you can set it so her movements activate the lights and music. It's great for encouraging kids to start moving their legs around. Come on; I'll show you where it is."

Tricia led them over to the bouncers and showed them the one she recommended. The blue seat was bright and decorated with marine life. A fish and a seahorse hung from the aquarium bar above the footrest. "This looks perfect," Srikkanth said. "We should just ask for you as soon as we walk in the door instead of trying to figure things out ourselves."

Tricia laughed. "I'm here to help if that's easier for you, but really, anyone at the store can help you with whatever you need. Let me help you get all this to the register and out to your car."

They got everything stowed in the back of the pickup truck Jaime had borrowed from a friend so they could take everything home. Right before Tricia turned back to the store, she gave them a big smile. "I'm glad I could see you all together as a family."

Srikkanth and Jaime both stared at her retreating back in stunned silence. A family?

Chapter Eight

A FULL week before Nathaniel moved out, Jaime already had his room packed and ready to move downstairs. He started moving his boxes in almost as soon as Nathaniel began moving his belongings out. Srikkanth watched the entire process with a bemused smile, amazed at how determined Jaime was to speed up the process of arranging Sophie's nursery. By the time Srikkanth started making dinner, Sophie's nursery was empty, ready for them to move her furniture in.

"Not tonight," Srikkanth insisted after dinner when Jaime started toward the storage shed outside where they'd put the boxes with Sophie's furniture. "We'll move her in tomorrow. It'll take too long to set up now."

"Are you sure?" Jaime asked. "I don't mind staying up to work on it so she can have her own space tonight."

"She'll be asleep long before we can get it done, and I don't want to wake her to move her later," Srikkanth demurred. "We'll work on it tomorrow. You're off again, right?"

Jaime nodded. "I managed to get two days off in a row this week. I knew we'd have a lot to do with moving everything around. Get her settled for the night then while I do the dishes. I guess it'll be every night chores now that there's just two of us."

"We can keep looking for a third roommate," Srikkanth offered.

"I wasn't complaining," Jaime replied quickly. "Just commenting." He bent to kiss Sophie where she was ensconced in Srikkanth's arms. "Good night, angel."

Jaime took his time doing the dishes. With all Sophie's bottles, they filled the dishwasher enough these days to make it worth using instead of simply washing their few dishes by hand. He loaded the dishwasher and set it to run before taking care of the pans from dinner. There was no reason to rush while Srikkanth was taking care of the baby. Eventually he got her settled and came back into the kitchen. "I've been thinking," Jaime began.

"Always dangerous," Srikkanth quipped.

Jaime scowled. "I've been in my room upstairs for over three years. I think we should paint the walls before we move Sophie in. They're white, so we can probably get away with just one coat, maybe the pale green that's in her comforter set. We can do that in the morning and then set everything up in the afternoon while it dries. We'll have to see how the fumes are, but even if she can't sleep in there tomorrow night, the room will be ready and she can move in the night after."

Srikkanth laughed. "The next thing you know, you'll want to put wallpaper up too."

"Not wallpaper," Jaime promised, "although I did see a really cute border with animals on it that would go with her sheets."

"No," Srikkanth replied emphatically. "No wallpaper, no border. We can paint the room—you're probably right about it needing a fresh coat—but that's plenty for now. When she's a little older, she can decide if she wants something else."

"All right, fine," Jaime agreed with a joking huff. "Can we at least agree on a color of paint?"

"I like the yellow in her quilt," Srikkanth said. "We can go by Home Depot in the morning and get them to match it, and we'll have the room painted by noon. If it needs a second coat, we could probably even do that tomorrow night and then move her in on Sunday."

"Sounds like a plan." Jaime got up from the table and headed into the living room, Srikkanth trailing behind him. He flopped down on the couch, staring blindly at the blank TV screen.

"Tired?" Jaime asked.

"Yeah," Srikkanth admitted.

"You need to relax," Jaime decided. "Let's watch a movie. Even if you fall asleep in the middle of it, that's okay."

"No, it's not," Srikkanth insisted. "If I fall asleep down here, I won't hear Sophie during the night."

He wouldn't be getting up with Sophie tonight one way or another, Jaime decided, looking at Srikkanth's drawn face. Jaime would take bottle duty tonight. "So I'll sleep upstairs and you can actually get a full night's sleep," he proposed.

"I couldn't possibly—"

"Yes, you could," Jaime interrupted. "Now, what do you want to watch? We've got sci-fi thrillers, stupid comedies, or war epics."

"Stupid comedies," Srikkanth said. "Definitely stupid comedies. I don't have any brain cells left to spare on anything more complicated than Jim Carrey or Robin Williams."

"Robin Williams it is then," Jaime declared. "Not even for you will I watch Jim Carrey. Unless it's in *The Truman Show*. Maybe."

Srikkanth chuckled. "Sophisticate. Just put on a movie. I'll be asleep in ten minutes anyway."

Jaime pulled out *Night at the Museum* and popped it in the DVD player. As he'd predicted, Srikkanth was asleep almost before the film itself started.

Jaime leaned back against the arm of the couch, his feet stretched out almost to Srikkanth's side, and marveled at the changes in his life over the past two months. His days of going out cruising every Friday night, with or without a date, seemed eons ago, even if he knew it was only a matter of weeks. He could still go. Srikkanth hadn't asked him to stay at the condo every night he didn't have to work, but Jaime found the club scene had suddenly lost its attraction. He wanted to be right where he was: at home watching Srikkanth sleep.

And if that wasn't a bitch of a realization, he didn't know what was. When they'd first decided to move in together, they'd made a pact not to date each other or any of their other roommates so they wouldn't bring that kind of drama into their home. It hadn't seemed like a big deal at the time. Sure, Srikkanth was attractive, but there were plenty of other attractive gay guys who didn't come with the added tension of living together. It had been easy, for three years, to pretend he hadn't noticed Sri. He might have continued like that forever if Sophie hadn't come into their lives. He could pretend not to notice Sri, but he couldn't pretend where Sophie was concerned.

THE next day, they went to Home Depot, Sophie's quilt in hand, and found a salesperson willing to help them match the color. He also armed them with rollers and brushes and pans and drop cloths, everything they would need, he said, to paint the nursery for their baby.

Once again, the reference caught Srikkanth off guard, but he didn't want to embarrass Jaime by saying anything about it in front of the employee, and bringing it up later felt far too awkward, even between friends. He decided letting it go was easier. After all, it didn't matter if Tricia or the Home Depot employee thought they were together. He'd had it happen multiple times when he was out places with Jill, even before she got pregnant. Once she was showing, it happened even more frequently. They'd gotten a good laugh out of it more than once. Except Srikkanth didn't want to get a laugh out of it this time, he realized as they paid and started home. He wanted it to be real. That wasn't going to happen, though, so he pushed the thought aside and focused on navigating the busy traffic.

The last thing he wanted was to get in an accident because he was distracted by thoughts of Jaime and have Sophie or Jaime get hurt.

Sophie gurgled and kicked her little feet in her bouncer as Jaime and Srikkanth painted her room. They laughed as they worked, music playing as they teased each other and tickled the baby. Srikkanth could almost believe they were a family at moments like this. He knew Jaime wasn't thinking in those terms. His friend had always avoided entanglements, preferring not to make promises he didn't know if he could keep. Srikkanth respected that forthright attitude, so he knew not to expect more from Jaime than he already had. A best friend and help with the baby was already a pretty good deal. He'd be greedy to ask for more.

They had worked for an hour, getting the room almost done, when Sophie got fussy. "I'll get her if you want," Jaime offered. "I'm done with the walls. All that's left is the edging."

"Thanks," Srikkanth said, trying to keep his hand steady as he painted along the baseboards. "Leave the roller. I'll wash it out when I'm done here. I don't think the room will need a second coat."

"I think you're right," Jaime agreed, wiping his hands on a damp rag so he wouldn't get paint on Sophie's clothes. Glancing down, he realized he had paint blobs on the front of his sweatshirt. He stripped it off and tossed it aside before picking Sophie up, cooing to her as he left the room.

"Shit," Srikkanth muttered under his breath as he watched Jaime and Sophie disappear down the stairs. "Get yourself under control, Bhattacharya," he scolded. "Jaime is not interested in you."

That didn't make Srikkanth less interested in Jaime, his body's reaction to the sight of that golden back undeniable as he shifted so the seam of his jeans wouldn't cut quite so deeply. "Good roommates are even harder to find than a good lay," he reminded himself firmly. "Don't screw up the best thing that ever happened to you by bringing sex into the equation. It isn't worth it."

Downstairs, Jaime mixed Sophie's bottle and set it in the warmer to heat, rocking her against him to distract her while he waited. *"Hush, little baby, don't say a word, Papa's gonna buy you a mockingbird.* Is that what you're going to call Sri?" he asked Sophie. "Is he going to be Papa or Daddy, or do Indian children call their fathers something else entirely?"

Obviously, Sophie didn't reply, but it did stop her crying at least, and that was far more important to Jaime than any response. He could ask Srikkanth about it later. He hadn't ever heard Sri refer to himself by any particular name. He ought to remind him to do that so she'd learn how to address him. The warmer clicked off, signaling the bottle was hot, and Jaime let everything else go as he sat at the table and rocked her while she ate. When she was done, he burped her gently and smiled as her eyes started to close. *"And if that mockingbird don't sing, Papa's gonna buy you a diamond ring."*

He carried her up the stairs to the playpen where she would sleep for another few hours until they could get her crib set up and her room aired out. Shutting the door behind him once he knew she was settled, he went back into the nursery.

"I know it's cold outside, but we really ought to open the windows so the paint fumes can clear out before we have Sophie sleep in here," he commented.

"You'll freeze to death if we open the windows and you don't have shirt on," Srikkanth teased.

Jaime chuckled. "I wasn't planning on standing around shirtless all day. Unless you'd prefer it that way."

He would, but Srikkanth wasn't about to tell Jaime that. "Just put some clothes on and I'll open the windows. We'll probably work up a sweat carrying in and setting up all her furniture anyway."

Jaime nodded. "Let me get a clean sweatshirt and I'll meet you downstairs. We can clean up the paintbrushes and then start moving furniture."

"Sounds good."

Jaime walked back downstairs to his new room, wondering about the fact that Srikkanth had noticed he was shirtless and cared enough to say something about it, even teasingly. He knew what he wanted the observation to mean, but he didn't figure it was terribly realistic. They'd been very clear about their boundaries when they'd moved in together. Still, a man could hope, couldn't he? Pulling a clean sweatshirt over his head, he went out into the kitchen to help Sri clean up.

"DAMN, this armoire is heavy," Jaime grunted as they maneuvered the piece of furniture up the stairs.

"It's solid cherry," Srikkanth reminded him, his voice strained as they pushed and pulled on the box, trying to get it up to Sophie's nursery. "Maybe we should've bought something cheaper."

With a final heave, they pushed the chest into the upstairs hallway. "If we had, we'd only end up replacing it in a couple of years," Jaime reminded him. "Yes, it's heavy, but it's good quality. And it's the biggest piece. The rest should be easier."

Srikkanth wasn't sure about that, but they'd see how it went. He grabbed his utility knife and cut away the cardboard box around the armoire so they could position it in one corner of Sophie's bedroom. Another trip brought up the chest of drawers that also doubled as a changing table. They brought up the bed on the final trip, setting out all the pieces so they could assemble it.

"This is going to be one of those projects that takes forever, isn't it?" Jaime groused.

"It might be," Srikkanth shrugged, "but Sophie will be far more comfortable here than in that little napper. I can't believe she's almost outgrown it already. She's only two months old."

"Babies grow fast," Jaime said. "And she's eating well, so there's no reason she shouldn't. I think I remember reading that most babies double their weight by the time they're six months old."

Srikkanth shook his head. "We'll have to get new clothes for her before long."

"Let's see if the ones she has will last until it warms up a little more. That way we can buy spring and summer things in the next size. They'll last longer that way."

"Makes sense."

They spread the directions out on the floor and started assembling the bed, attaching the side rails to the headboard and footboard with long screws and then positioning the bedsprings at the highest level so they could reach her easily while still supporting her head. Finally, they got the bed together and the sheets on the mattress. "I think everything's ready," Jaime declared. "Now she just needs to wake up so we can show her her new room."

As if on cue, Sophie started fussing in the other room. Laughing, the two men went into Srikkanth's bedroom. "You do the honors," Jaime said. "She's your daughter."

"Come here, Sophie," Srikkanth said with a smile, picking her up. "Do you want to see the room Uncle Jaime and I made for you?"

"What's she going to call you?" Jaime interrupted.

"Daddy," Srikkanth said, eyes tearing up as he thought about the unexpected blessing.

"Call yourself Daddy when you're talking to her so she knows who you are," Jaime suggested. "That's the way babies learn names."

"Do you want to see the room Uncle Jaime and Daddy made for you?" Srikkanth repeated, the appellation awkward on his tongue, but he'd get used to it. Eventually.

Srikkanth carried her into the nursery, Jaime trailing behind him, not wanting to intrude on the moment between father and daughter, but Srikkanth didn't let him hang back for long, gesturing him into the room. "What do you think, *betti*?" he asked. "Do you like it? Uncle Jaime picked out the sheets and quilt. They'll keep you nice and warm for the rest of the winter, and then we'll get something lighter for you during the summer."

"Your daddy picked out the furniture, though," Jaime told her. "He wanted something nice for you. Something you could use even when you were older. Don't grow up too fast, though, baby girl. Let us enjoy you a little while longer, okay?"

Sophie gurgled at them again, her little hands reaching for both familiar faces. They leaned down to let her touch, their foreheads bumping as they did. "Sorry," Jaime apologized, straightening back up. He looked anywhere but at Srikkanth to hide his embarrassment and his desire.

"Don't worry about it," Srikkanth said hoarsely. "It was just a little bump."

The nursery finished, they went back downstairs to fix dinner. Jaime took one look in the fridge and groaned. "Chinese?"

"Sure," Srikkanth laughed. "Anything to avoid having to cook and do dishes tonight."

Jaime laughed and called in their usual order, changing clothes again so he wouldn't scare anyone when he went to pick up the food.

AFTER dinner, Srikkanth tucked Sophie into her new bed, hovering in the doorway even after she was asleep.

"Come downstairs," Jaime insisted. "We can finish watching the movie you missed last night. We got the monitor set up. You'll be able to hear her if she wakes up."

"All right," Srikkanth conceded finally, although he found it difficult to pull away from the door. His little girl was growing up.

Once he got settled, though, the movie got his attention, and he watched it all the way through to the end. Sophie woke up hungry just as the credits started to roll.

"Perfect timing," Jaime laughed. "Go get her. I'll bring up a bottle."

Srikkanth went up to the nursery, picking Sophie up and rocking her in the new glider. "This is much nicer than being cramped in Daddy's room, isn't it, Sophie? Uncle Jaime's getting you a bottle. You can fill your little tummy and then go back to bed in your big comfortable crib."

"Here you go," Jaime said softly from the doorway.

Srikkanth held his hand out. Jaime brought it to him and then left the two of them alone again.

Srikkanth gave Sophie the bottle and rocked gently as she drank. The repetitive motion soothed him as much as it did his daughter, and before long, he fell asleep holding her.

When Srikkanth didn't come back downstairs, even to say goodnight like he usually did, Jaime wandered back upstairs. The sight that met his eyes nearly took him to his knees, so strong was his desire to be a part of the tableau. Srikkanth sat in the glider still, his head back against the headrest, his feet on the ottoman. Sophie lay in his arms, sound asleep, the forgotten bottle hanging loosely from Srikkanth's limp hand. Jaime debated what to do. He could try to get her into her own bed, but he risked waking both of them if he did. He could wake Srikkanth and let him put Sophie in bed, but Srikkanth was obviously exhausted. Slipping into Srikkanth's room, Jaime pulled the heavy comforter off the bed, carrying it back into Sophie's room and draping it over both of them, careful to make sure her face was completely unobscured. "Sleep well," he whispered, bending to kiss her forehead softly. Feeling daring, he ghosted his lips across Srikkanth's forehead as well, catching a whiff of cologne as he did.

He left them to sleep, resolving to come up with a better solution than Srikkanth sleeping upright in the rocker. It might be all right for tonight, but it would give him neck cramps for sure if he did it very often.

CHAPTER NINE

"SOMETHING'S wrong with Sophie," Srikkanth said as soon as Jaime walked in the door from work. "She hasn't stopped crying all day, and she's rubbing at her ear."

"Does she have a fever?" Jaime asked, crossing to Srikkanth's side and laying his hand on Sophie's forehead. "She feels hot."

"She's been like that all day," Srikkanth verified.

"I think we need to take her to the doctor," Jaime said. "She obviously isn't well. Do you want me to call and make an appointment?"

"Would you take her instead?" Srikkanth asked, knowing his voice was pitiful but unable to care. He was exhausted from listening to Sophie cry all day. "I'll call the doctor."

"Of course," Jaime said, scooping Sophie out of Srikkanth's arms and rocking her against his chest. "It's going to be all right, *mi hija*," he crooned. "Daddy's going to take you to the doctor, and we're going to get you all fixed up. Just relax and hang on a little bit longer."

Srikkanth came back into the room a few minutes later. "They have an opening in an hour," he told Jaime. "They said it sounded like an ear infection."

"At least they can see her today," Jaime said, rocking Sophie soothingly. "Why don't you go take a shower, get something to eat, just take a break? I can hold her until it's time to go."

Srikkanth was ridiculously grateful. Summoning a tired smile, he went back downstairs to eat. It had been a hideous day, not knowing what to do to help Sophie, afraid she was sick but not sure it wasn't another bout of colic. Granted, she hadn't had one in awhile, but that didn't mean she'd never have another one. Several times, he'd started to pick up the phone and call Jaime, but that felt too much like admitting defeat.

Or admitting the other feelings he'd developed for his friend. He was afraid to admit that even more than he was to admit he needed help. After all, anyone could need help, and they'd already established that he had no idea what he was doing where Sophie was concerned. Things had gotten better, obviously. He knew how to deal with the daily routine now, but her crying today hadn't been routine. He'd never been so glad to see someone as he was to see Jaime when he came home today.

With a sigh, Srikkanth headed to the shower, needing the hot water to help him relax. Maybe he'd jerk off while he was in there. He couldn't remember the last time he'd come. Certainly before Sophie was born. He couldn't very well jerk off with her sleeping in the same room, and all of his showers had been rushed, not knowing how long she'd sleep and not wanting her to wake and cry for him while he was bathing. Now, knowing she was safe in Jaime's arms, no matter how upset, he could relax for a bit and let go. If nothing else, it would put him in a better frame of mind for whatever the doctor had to say.

Stripping down, he climbed beneath the hot spray, letting the water soothe away his fatigue. He took his time washing his hair, the feel of it brushing his shoulders a reminder that he hadn't had a haircut since before Sophie was born either. It wouldn't be too much longer before he'd have to go back to work. Maybe he ought to see if Jaime would mind watching her for an hour or two one evening so he could visit the barber.

Thinking about Jaime brought back his other mission in the shower. Leaning against the shower wall, he closed his eyes and summoned an image of his sexy roommate the way he'd seen him yesterday, shirtless and sweaty. In his fantasy, Jaime wasn't walking away from him to get Sophie, but rather walking toward him with intent. Srikkanth shivered despite the heat of the water, imagining Jaime's elegant features transformed with lust. God, he wanted to see that.

His hand drifted lower, across his abdomen and down to his cock. Circling it with his fist, he stroked leisurely, letting the tension build as he pictured Jaime in the shower with him, imagined it was Jaime's hand on his cock and Jaime's cock in his hand. He shuddered at the burst of need that spun through him at the thought. He'd never let himself do this. He had always refused to violate their agreement even in his mind, but he couldn't seem to stop himself now. He needed release, and none of the men he'd slept with in the past, none of the models he'd ogled on occasion, would do it for him now. His thoughts had one target and one target only: Jaime.

As if that realization triggered something within him, Srikkanth's hand sped up, shuttling up and down on his sensitive shaft, pushing him closer and closer to release. He lifted his other hand to his mouth, biting into his palm to muffle the sound he made as he came, though he hoped the water helped as well. His cock twitched hard in his hand, semen jetting out to coat the wall of the enclosure. Feeling guilty for dreaming of Jaime when Jaime was taking care of Sophie, Srikkanth finished bathing and turned off the water. Drying off, he tried to regain his composure, not wanting Jaime to realize what he'd done in the shower. Even if he didn't assume Srikkanth had been fantasizing about him, that wasn't why Jaime was watching the baby. He'd agreed to watch her so Srikkanth could get ready to go to the doctor's office.

Finally ready, Srikkanth went back to the nursery. Sophie had settled a little in Jaime's arms, whimpering pitifully instead of screaming bloody murder. It was a small consolation, at least. "Shall we go?" Srikkanth asked. "It's a bit of a drive to the pediatrician's."

"Do you want me to come with you?" Jaime asked, surprised.

"Please," Srikkanth said. "I'm afraid I'll miss half of what the doctor says, and I don't want to mess up his instructions. I want Sophie to get well as quickly as possible."

"Okay," Jaime agreed with a pleased smile.

They spent the drive to the doctor's office trying to soothe Sophie, to no avail. Fortunately, they didn't have to wait long in the waiting room, the nurse calling them back into the exam room right away. "What are you in here for today?" the nurse asked.

"Sophie's fussy. She feels hot, like she's running a fever. She hasn't eaten well today or slept hardly at all," Srikkanth explained.

"She's also been pulling at her ear," Jaime chimed in.

"And when did this start?" the nurse inquired.

"This morning," Srikkanth replied.

"After I left for work," Jaime added. "She wasn't fussy during the night or early this morning."

"But not long after," Srikkanth continued, "so it's probably been since a little after nine."

"Let me take her temperature," the nurse said. "We'll start with that, and then the doctor can go from there."

The nurse approached with a thermometer, the pressure against Sophie's ear as she took the baby's temperature enough to set her screaming again. "One hundred point four," the nurse declared after a moment, "and her ear is definitely sensitive. Most babies don't even notice the thermometer unless they have an ear infection. Go ahead and take her top off so the doctor can listen to her chest as well, to make sure she doesn't have anything else. He'll be with you in a moment. She's a lovely baby, gentlemen. Did you adopt her?"

"No, she's my daughter," Srikkanth replied, caught off guard yet again by the assumption he and Jaime were a couple. "Her mother died in childbirth."

"Oh, I'm sorry," the nurse apologized. "We've just seen so many couples with adopted children recently that I naturally assumed...."

"It's fine," Srikkanth assured her. "A perfectly logical mistake. We'll wait for the doctor."

Flustered, the nurse left them alone. "That's the third person in as many weeks," Jaime chuckled, choosing to focus on the humor in the situation rather than on how much he wished the nurse were right.

Before Srikkanth could decide how to reply to that, the doctor knocked and came in. "Mr. Bhattacharya, how are you?" Sophie chose that moment to let out another wail.

"I've been better," Srikkanth admitted. "Sophie is sick."

"So I hear," the doctor replied. "Let me take a look at her."

Jaime stepped back to make room for the doctor, who listened carefully to her heart and lungs. "Her lungs sound clear. That's good. Has she had a cold or seemed congested?"

"Not really," Srikkanth replied. "I mean, I've wiped her nose a couple of times, but I figured that was because she was crying so much. She's barely stopped all day."

"Let me check her ears," the doctor said. "That's probably what's causing all this. If it is an ear infection, she won't like this. Hold her so she doesn't squirm."

Srikkanth tightened his grip as the doctor approached with the otoscope.

As predicted, Sophie started screaming pretty much the moment the exam tool touched her ear. The doctor was obviously used to the sound, though, taking his time to examine her ear thoroughly. "It's not as bad as all that," the doctor soothed when he stepped back. "She definitely has an infection in that ear. Let me check the other one to see how it's doing, and then I'll give you a prescription for some amoxicillin to clear it up."

"Do you have to check the other ear when you already know she needs medicine?" Srikkanth asked, not sure he could stand listening to her scream that way again.

"It's better to know for her records," the doctor explained. "If she's prone to ear infections on one side, the other side, or both sides, it may change the long-term treatment options. I know it's hard. Maybe let your partner hold her for this one. That way you won't feel quite so guilty about letting me check her out."

There it was again. That automatic assumption he and Jaime were a couple. The suggestion made sense, though, so he handed Sophie to Jaime. The doctor waited until Sophie was settled in Jaime's arms before checking her other ear. "This one's clear," he said. "That's good. It means we caught the infection early. She'll still need a course of antibiotics, but hopefully she'll recover more quickly and not be as fractious in the meantime." He sat down at the desk and pulled out his scrip pad. "How old is she now?"

"Two and a half months," Srikkanth replied.

The doctor nodded and wrote out the prescription. "And she can have a half dropper of infant Tylenol or Motrin every six hours. If that isn't enough, you can alternate between the two of them every three hours, as long as it's six hours between each dose of the same medicine. The hardest part of an ear infection for babies her age is the pain. The antibiotic can take up to thirty-six hours to start working, and you obviously don't want to listen to her scream for that long. The painkiller will help with the fever as well, and that should help her get her appetite back. If she isn't noticeably better in forty-eight hours, call us back. If her fever goes higher than one-oh-three, bring her back in or take her to an urgent care center if it's after-hours. None of that should happen now that she's on antibiotics, but I prefer to give all the precautions rather than take chances."

Srikkanth could feel his eyes glazing over with all the information.

"Don't worry," Jaime said softly. "I've got it. Let's go get her the medicine she needs so she can start feeling better."

"Thank you," Srikkanth said to the doctor. "We really appreciate you seeing us on such short notice today."

"We always leave slots open for sick patients," the doctor assured him. "Nothing's worse than having your baby ill and not being able to get her seen. When my children were her age, not everyone was as careful about it, and I remember taking my daughter to the emergency room for something that should have been treated by her doctor, except we couldn't get an appointment. I swore I'd never do that to my patients when I had a practice of my own."

"We're grateful," Jaime said, handing Srikkanth back to Sophie and pulling on his coat.

They dropped the prescription off at the pharmacy to be filled and went in search of the analgesics the doctor had recommended. By the time they found those and picked up a few other things Sophie needed, the prescription was ready.

Back at home, they gave Sophie her medicine and waited anxiously for the Tylenol to do its job so she could rest. They could tell the moment it did, because she fell asleep almost instantly.

"I'll put her to bed," Srikkanth said, his voice betraying his fatigue.

"Why don't you lie down for a few minutes too?" Jaime suggested. "It'll take me at least half an hour to make dinner."

"Do you mind?" Srikkanth asked.

"Of course not," Jaime insisted. "Go on."

Srikkanth carried Sophie upstairs and put her in her bed, collapsing onto the daybed that had appeared in her nursery two days after they'd set it up. "You'll give yourself a perpetual backache if you keep sleeping in the rocker," Jaime had teased him by way of explanation. Srikkanth had been touched by the generous gift, though he tried to use it sparingly so he wouldn't spoil Sophie completely by always sleeping in the room with her. After all, what was the point of setting up a nursery if he was still going to sleep with her?

Now, though, worried about her because of the ear infection, the daybed was a godsend. He could rest but be close to hear her if she needed him. In a matter of seconds, he was sound asleep.

Downstairs, Jaime took his time making dinner when he didn't hear any footsteps. Srikkanth was visibly tired, and Jaime didn't feel any rush to wake him. His thoughts raced as his hands worked automatically to cut the mushrooms for the cream of mushroom soup recipe his mother had given him. Every time he and Sri went out with Sophie, people assumed they were a family. He certainly wanted that to be true, but he'd assumed Srikkanth would want to hold to their original bargain. He hadn't given any indication otherwise. Except in all the little things that seemed to proclaim them as a couple to everyone else. He leaned on Jaime for support and advice where Sophie was concerned. They shared a house, chores, financial burdens. Everything except the closeness and comfort that could come from a loving relationship.

He found Srikkanth attractive. He liked him. He loved Sophie. That seemed like a pretty decent foundation on which to build a relationship. Maybe after dinner, he could find a way to broach the subject.

Half an hour later, the soup was ready. He left it on low heat so it wouldn't get cold while he went to find Srikkanth. He tapped lightly on Srikkanth's door, but his roommate didn't answer. Frowning, he pushed the door ajar and looked inside, but the bed was empty. Shaking his head, he went next door to Sophie's room, finding Srikkanth asleep on the daybed. "You're going to spoil her," he murmured as he went to Srikkanth's side, perching on the edge of the bed, his hand shaking Srikkanth's shoulder gently. "Sri," he whispered, leaning close so he wouldn't disturb Sophie.

The dark eyes fluttered open, luminous in the near darkness, vulnerable, needy, a little afraid but relieved when recognition set in. The combination was more than Jaime could resist. He lowered his head that little bit more and brushed his lips across Srikkanth's, sure as he did that he'd end up on his ass on the bedroom floor, but Srikkanth didn't pull away. His eyes closed again slowly as his lips moved with languid ease beneath Jaime's, welcoming the kiss, welcoming Jaime. A soft sigh escaped Srikkanth's lips, ghosting across Jaime's mouth. Jaime lifted his head for a moment, waiting for Srikkanth's eyes to open again. When they did, he raised an eyebrow in silent question. Srikkanth's answer was equally silent but absolutely unequivocal as he pulled Jaime back down for another kiss, a longer, more intense one this time, their noses bumping as they worked around the awkward angle.

"Let me sit up," Srikkanth whispered.

Jaime moved back, giving Srikkanth room. Sophie stirred restlessly in her bed, so Jaime reached for Srikkanth's hand, drawing him out into the hallway. "Let's go downstairs where we won't disturb the baby."

Srikkanth followed docilely, still too surprised by the kiss and befuddled from sleep to process what had just happened. When they reached the kitchen and Jaime urged him toward the table, Srikkanth stopped and turned to face his roommate.

"Is this because of Sophie?"

"Of course not," Jaime said, offended Srikkanth could think such a thing. "I love Sophie, yes, because she's a sweet, engaging baby, but I don't need to put the moves on you in order to be a part of her life, as you well know since she's ten weeks old already. This is because of you and me."

"Sorry," Srikkanth apologized. "Everything's so crazy right now. I'm afraid. My thoughts are all mixed up in my head, and I don't know what I'm doing half the time. The other half, I'm asleep."

Jaime laughed. "Don't be afraid. I know the thought of raising a child alone is daunting, but you don't have to be alone. Let me help."

"You're already doing so much," Srikkanth protested.

Jaime shook his head. "Let me take care of you too."

Srikkanth didn't know what to say. The longing for a true partner, not simply someone to help him take care of Sophie, but someone to lean on for himself, was undeniably strong.

"Come on, Sri," Jaime urged. "What can it hurt?"

Srikkanth could think of all kinds of things, all the reasons they'd agreed not to get involved with each other when they decided to become roommates, but all of that paled in comparison to the way Jaime looked at Sophie every time he picked her up, the way he was looking at Srikkanth now.

"All right. We'll give it a try."

Smiling widely, content with the world at the moment, Jaime stepped closer to Srikkanth, enfolding him in a tender embrace. He brushed his lips across Srikkanth's again, trying to invest the contact with all the tenderness and affection he could muster. Srikkanth returned the gesture in kind, finally resting their foreheads together in comfortable silence.

CHAPTER TEN

TWO days before Srikkanth was due to go back to work, the phone rang. Srikkanth didn't recognize the number, but he answered it anyway. "Hello?"

"Hello, I know it's been awhile, but I just found your ad about a room to rent. I was wondering if it was still available."

The question made Srikkanth smile even as he apologized and explained that the room had already been occupied. Jaime came in as he was finishing the call. He stretched out his arm in welcome, turning to nuzzle Jaime's neck as soon as he hung up the phone. The empty room had been filled perfectly.

"Who was that?" Jaime asked curiously.

"Someone wanting to rent our spare room if it was still available," Srikkanth replied. "I told him it had been taken." He tipped his head up for a kiss. "I told him it was taken. I didn't tell him I'd found the perfect situation."

"Perfect?" Jaime teased.

"Absolutely," Srikkanth insisted. "I have a daughter I love, a roommate who loves her as much as I do, and a man in my life who takes as good care of me as he does of her. What isn't perfect about that?"

"Well, when you put it that way," Jaime agreed, leaning closer to kiss Srikkanth more deeply. Their tongues had barely touched when Sophie cried out in the next room.

"She's hungry," Srikkanth apologized.

"I'll get her," Jaime offered. "You've had her all day."

"Yeah, but I have to go back to work in two days. I want all the time with her I can get," Srikkanth replied, going into the other room and bringing Sophie back as Jaime prepared her bottle.

"Any news on whether they'll let you work from home?" Jaime asked when Sophie was settled.

"They approved it today, but only four days a week. I have to go in on Mondays," Srikkanth explained. "I don't know what I'm going to do then."

"That's easy," Jaime said. "I'm the manager at my store. I'll simply take Sunday and Monday off instead of Saturday and Sunday. We'll still have one day off together, and I can watch Sophie on Monday while you're at work."

"You don't mind?" Srikkanth asked, ridiculously grateful for Jaime's offer.

"Not at all," Jaime replied. "It really doesn't matter to me one way or another which days I take off as long as we have some time together. And this gives me some extra time with Sophie too. Most importantly, it helps you out."

"I'm not sure what I did to deserve you," Srikkanth said, "but I'm glad you're here. I can't possibly say thank you enough."

Jaime ended that conversation with a kiss. He wasn't interested in Srikkanth's gratitude, only his heart. Srikkanth was holding Sophie between them, making a deeper kiss impossible, but Jaime found he didn't even mind. She was as much a part of this as they were. Jaime would never have crossed their self-imposed boundaries without her.

"I've already done the schedule for next week, but I'll see if I can switch days with someone. Worst-case scenario, I'll take a sick day. I never come close to using them," Jaime offered.

"I know you don't want to hear it, but thank you," Srikkanth repeated. "I couldn't do this without you."

"Yes, you could," Jaime insisted. "You'd simply find other solutions to the problems. I'm glad to help, though. You know how much I enjoy being with Sophie and you."

Srikkanth wasn't sure which of those statements pleased him more. He'd be lost without Jaime's help where Sophie was concerned, but he'd come to rely nearly as much on Jaime's affection for him. Holding Sophie in his arms thrilled him in a way he'd never known before, but the need for companionship was one she couldn't fulfill. Jaime took care of that one beyond all his imaginings, and all they'd done so far was kiss.

Lots of kisses. Slow, tender kisses, hard, passionate kisses. Hot and heavy with lots of tongue that lasted for what seemed like hours. Soft and sweet and over before they started. Srikkanth didn't think he'd ever been kissed the way Jaime kissed him, and that was a truly wonderful thing.

TEARING off his tie, Srikkanth hurried up the sidewalk to the house. Work hadn't been bad, but nine hours away from Sophie was eight and a half hours too many. Rationally, he knew Sophie wouldn't forget him in that amount of time or hate him for leaving her with Jaime, but the churning in his stomach all day and the empty feeling in his heart had nothing to do with rationality and everything to do with missing his daughter.

Jaime opened the door as Srikkanth stepped onto the porch, Sophie in his arms. Before Srikkanth could even open his mouth, Jaime had put Sophie in his arms. She gurgled happily, and all the stress of the day disappeared as her little arms went around his neck. He took a deep breath, taking in the scent of baby lotion and fresh powder and Sophie. "How did you know what I needed?"

Jaime smiled and leaned in for a quick kiss. "Because I look forward to coming home and seeing her every day too," Jaime explained. "Come inside and relax. Dinner will be ready in about half an hour."

"You're spoiling me," Srikkanth protested. "It was my night to cook."

"So what?" Jaime asked. "You worked today and I didn't. You can cook tomorrow and the next day if you want, but I really don't mind."

Srikkanth kissed Jaime again, toeing his shoes off at the front door as he carried Sophie into the living room and sat on the couch. "How are you, *betti*? Did you have a good day with Jaime?"

She didn't reply, of course, but she bounced on Srikkanth's knee, waving her arms enthusiastically and tracking his movement with bright eyes.

"After dinner, we should take Sophie for a walk," Jaime suggested. "It's staying light longer and isn't as cold. We could all use an outing."

"That's a good idea," Srikkanth replied. "I'll go change and find her jacket so we can go as soon as we're done eating."

An hour later, dinner finished and the dishes in the dishwasher, they set Sophie in her stroller and went out for a walk. The evening air was brisk, but not bitter, so they stopped at the park down the street, taking Sophie out of her stroller so she could look around more easily.

"This'll be a story to tell the grandkids," Jaime joked. "Our first date was a walk in the park with Sophie a chaperone."

"I'm taking terrible advantage of your generosity," Srikkanth lamented.

"I remember offering multiple times," Jaime pointed out. "I want to be right where I am, on a park bench in the middle of April with you and Sophie. Nobody forced me to be here."

"You deserve a real courtship," Srikkanth insisted, "not stolen moments when Sophie isn't demanding my attention."

"No, I deserve a real family," Jaime countered, "and that's what we're building, one slow, tender kiss at a time."

"Is that really how you see us?" Srikkanth asked, stomach jumping with nerves.

"We're sitting in a park with a baby and a diaper bag and all the rest," Jaime laughed. "What else would you call it?"

Srikkanth laughed as well. "Okay, point taken. It's getting a little chilly sitting here. Let's keep walking."

Jaime took Sophie and tucked her back in her stroller, making sure the blankets were tucked snugly around her. She cooed happily at him, bringing a big grin to his face. "Could she be any sweeter?"

"I don't know how," Srikkanth replied with a grin. He smiled even bigger when Jaime put one hand over his on the handle of the stroller.

SRIKKANTH sighed and stretched on the couch, working out the kinks of the day. He always felt like he hunched more when he was working at the office. The chair wasn't as comfortable. The desk wasn't quite the right height. Not only was it better for Sophie if he worked from home, it was better for him.

"Stiff?" Jaime asked from the armchair next to him.

"Yeah," Srikkanth replied. "My back is all tensed up."

"Lie down," Jaime directed. "On your stomach so I can work on your back."

Quirking an eyebrow, Srikkanth did as Jaime directed, stretching out flat on his stomach. Jaime rose and crossed to his side. "This will be easier if I straddle you," he said. "Is that all right?"

"You just want to get me beneath you," Srikkanth joked.

Jaime snorted. "If that's all I wanted, I'd have snuck into your bed weeks ago."

"Why didn't you?" Srikkanth retorted.

"Because I want more than that," Jaime reminded him, hands settling on Srikkanth's shoulders even as he continued to talk. "I want it all. You, Sophie, me, a family. And that means taking our time and doing this right so we make it work rather than rushing into bed and screwing everything up later."

When Srikkanth didn't reply, Jaime turned his attention to the stiff muscles in Srikkanth's shoulders. He wasn't worried about the lack of reply now. Srikkanth had already agreed in so many better ways.

Srikkanth's eyes closed as Jaime worked over his back, massaging firmly up and down his spine, concentrating on his shoulders and the spot between his shoulder blades. He couldn't smother a little moan when he felt one of the knots suddenly give beneath the constant pressure.

"Feel good?" Jaime asked.

"God, yes," Srikkanth replied. "I didn't realize I'd gotten so tense."

"It was your first day back in the office after a long time off, your first day away from Sophie. I'd be surprised if you weren't tense," Jaime said.

"Yeah, and my desk at work isn't terribly comfortable," Srikkanth agreed. "I won't complain about working primarily from home for more reasons than just the time spent with Sophie."

"You could ask for another chair," Jaime laughed. "There's no reason to be miserable."

Srikkanth shrugged beneath the massage. "There's not much point now that I'm at home eighty percent of the time. They aren't going to want to spend any money on a desk that hardly gets used."

"You're at home four days a week now," Jaime agreed, "but you may not always be. Sophie will go to preschool eventually."

"Who knows where we'll be by then," Srikkanth said. "I may not even be with the same company. We'll just have to see how things go."

Jaime shook his head. "Fine. Then the first thing we do on Monday night after Sophie goes to bed is give you a massage so you don't end up sore the next day."

That sounded wonderful to Srikkanth. For the chance to relax and for the opportunity to feel Jaime's hands on him. He was coming to crave that the way he craved Sophie's smile. Eventually, Jaime's hands stilled. "You should go upstairs and get some sleep," he murmured in Srikkanth's ear. "You're exhausted."

Srikkanth roused himself from his near-doze, lifting his head. "Why don't you come upstairs with me?" he murmured, meeting Jaime's eyes. "My bed's big enough for both of us."

"Are you sure, Sri?" Jaime asked. "That's a big step, and I don't want you to feel rushed."

"Honestly, I'm probably too tired to do much other than sleep tonight," Srikkanth admitted, "but I'd like to do so with your arms around me and your warmth in bed next to me."

"Then I'd like nothing more," Jaime replied, slipping off the couch to kneel beside it so he could kiss Srikkanth deeply. "Let me get ready for bed and I'll join you upstairs. How does that sound?"

Srikkanth smiled. "Perfect."

Anticipation jangling along his nerves, Srikkanth hurried upstairs and into the bathroom, taking a few minutes to brush his teeth and wash his face and chest to freshen up a bit. He considered taking a quick shower, but he didn't want to spend that time or seem too eager for more when he'd already told Jaime he was too tired for much in the way of intimacy. His body had other ideas, but he didn't want to pressure Jaime. Besides, he really did want the comfort of someone next to him in the night.

Pulling on a pair of flannel sleep pants and his robe, Srikkanth walked into the bedroom to find the most tempting sight he'd seen in a long time. Jaime lay in his bed, bare-chested, a welcoming smile on his face. "Why aren't you freezing?" Srikkanth asked, shivering despite his robe.

"Because I'm thinking of you," Jaime replied with an impish grin. "Get in bed and I'll help warm you up."

Srikkanth shed his robe, his skin tingling in the cool room, and climbed into bed next to Jaime, gasping at the heat radiating off the other man's body. "You're a regular furnace!"

Jaime smiled. "I told you I'd warm you up."

Srikkanth snuggled closer, enjoying the heat of a body next to his and the sensation of skin against skin. Jaime's arms enclosed him in a welcoming embrace, eliciting a deep sigh from Srikkanth's chest.

"Tired?" Jaime asked.

"A little," Srikkanth replied, "but mostly happy to be here with you."

Jaime smiled against Srikkanth's hair. "I'm happy to be here too." His hands smoothed down the long muscles of Srikkanth's back in gentle imitation of the massage earlier in the evening.

Srikkanth hummed his pleasure, the sound too much of a temptation for Jaime. He tipped Srikkanth's head up so their mouths could meet as he repeated the caress, hoping for more of the encouraging noises. Srikkanth obliged, his lips parting with eager abandon, ceding control of the kiss to Jaime's skillful mastery. When his hands met fabric, Jaime debated for a moment slipping them beneath, but he decided not to, letting them coast lower on top of the cloth instead.

Srikkanth shifted closer still, aligning their bodies completely as he began his own explorations. Jaime was warm—hot—all over, his back beneath Srikkanth's hands as well as his chest pressed firmly against Srikkanth's front. Sri let his hands wander, imitating Jaime's caresses, reveling in the way Jaime moved against him, more intimate than all the eager kisses that had gone before. There was something about lying in bed with someone, kissing and caressing, that added depth to the movements, far more than standing in the kitchen or snuggling on the couch. Not that

Srikkanth had been this bold before now. He'd realized at the park today how much of a family they were becoming, and that gave him the courage—the freedom—to act as he was now.

He rolled to his back, drawing Jaime with him so the other man lay directly on top of him, his weight pushing Srikkanth into the mattress. He twined his fingers in Jaime's dark hair, drawing their lips together for a kiss, wondering where his fatigue had gone and how far they dared go tonight, when a cry in the other room had them jumping apart like guilty schoolboys.

Srikkanth glanced at the clock. "She's hungry," he apologized, getting up and reaching for his robe.

"I'll get the bottle and meet you in the nursery," Jaime offered. "I don't want you out of my sight for as long as it would take you to feed her by yourself."

Srikkanth grinned, his face glowing at the thought that Jaime desired his company to that extent. "Okay. Hurry."

Jaime nodded, taking the steps two at a time on his way down to get the bottle. Srikkanth pulled his robe on, not up to walking around bare-chested in the cool house, and went into the nursery, picking Sophie up and sitting on the daybed. Usually, he fed her in the rocking chair, but there wasn't room for both him and Jaime in the rocking chair. It would be snug even on the daybed. Two minutes later, Jaime came in with the bottle, handing it to Srikkanth and urging him to scoot toward the foot of the bed so Jaime could prop the pillows up. When they were arranged to his satisfaction, he reclined against them, pulled Srikkanth and Sophie into his arms, and drew the covers up over all three of them. "Warm enough?"

"Between you and Sophie, I'm nice and toasty," Srikkanth promised, watching Sophie as she gobbled down the formula. Her eyes closed quickly as the familiar routine lulled her back to sleep. Closing his eyes as well, Srikkanth let his head settle against Jaime's shoulder, reveling in the inner warmth evoked by their pose. He was pretty sure he'd be content to never move, although it would be hard to do much more than kiss Jaime sitting this way. Jaime wasn't so constrained, though, his hands free to wander other than where Srikkanth was holding Sophie.

She finished her bottle and Srikkanth tucked her back in bed, both of them bending to kiss her forehead before they left the room again, shutting the door quietly behind them.

"Shall we go back to bed?" Jaime asked.

Srikkanth shivered, not only from the cold.

"I think that's the best idea I've heard all night."

Chapter Eleven

Back in bed, they snuggled together again, Srikkanth's robe falling to the floor beneath Jaime's hands as he crowded Srikkanth from behind. "Eager?" Srikkanth teased.

"If you only knew," Jaime replied, nudging Srikkanth with his hips. He didn't make any move beyond that, however, much to Srikkanth's disappointment.

Srikkanth rolled into Jaime's arms, bringing as much of their bodies into contact as he could, his hands roving over his boyfriend's back. "Now where were we?"

"I don't know," Jaime teased in return. "You'll have to refresh my memory."

Srikkanth grinned and rolled onto his back again, pulling Jaime on top of him as they'd been before Sophie woke up. "Now let's hope the rest doesn't repeat itself."

"I hope she sleeps," Jaime agreed, "but you know it doesn't bother me that she needs you."

"Needs us," Srikkanth insisted. "I couldn't do this by myself, but more than that, I see her reacting to you the same way she reacts to me."

Jaime shrugged, a little worried Sri would feel like Jaime was trying to take his place as Sophie's father. "Close maybe, but she knows who her father is."

"I don't mind, if that's what you're thinking," Srikkanth said quickly. "Most babies have two parents to love and to love them.

I'm not losing anything by having her care for you too. I'm just glad you want to be a part of her life as well as of mine."

Jaime chuckled. "At this point, I don't see one being possible without the other. Besides, I'm the one who's the winner in this situation. I get a gorgeous boyfriend and an adorable child all in one swoop."

Srikkanth blushed, though he doubted it would show with his dark skin. It didn't stop the heat from rising in his face at Jaime's declaration. He slipped his arms around Jaime's neck and pulled his face down for a kiss. Their lips met gently, brushing back and forth, tender contact that reinforced Jaime's words. Srikkanth's impatience grew at the slow pace. His body clamored for more. He flicked his tongue over Jaime's lips, asking for more. Jaime's lips parted, welcoming him in, his tongue tangling with Srikkanth's, sharing one breath as the kiss deepened. Srikkanth ran his hands down Jaime's back, stopping at the waistband of his pajama bottoms. "May I?"

Jaime lifted his head, staring down into Srikkanth's eyes in the dim light of the lamp. "I don't want to rush this," he said slowly. "I want to take our time and savor every moment and take every step consciously rather than because we got swept away by our feelings. Just let me hold you tonight. That's enough for now. There will be time for more later, when everything isn't so new."

Disappointed, Srikkanth rolled from beneath Jaime's weight, but the other man's arms wound around him immediately, spooning them together, making it clear without words that his choice was a delay, not a rejection. Srikkanth relaxed into the embrace, sighing softly when Jaime nuzzled the back of his neck before pulling the covers over them so they would stay warm as they slept.

TWO days later, Srikkanth lay in wait for Jaime's return. Jaime had called to say he'd be late because of a problem at the store and not to try to keep Sophie up or to hold dinner. Srikkanth had put Sophie to bed at her normal time—he'd already figured out the importance of keeping her routine as regular as possible—but he'd stuck dinner back in the fridge and settled for a quick snack for himself to tide him over until Jaime got home. The thought of eating alone was completely unappealing. He'd rather wait for Jaime, even if it meant being hungry, than eat by himself. Instead, he'd dug out a jar of peanuts and munched on them to take the edge off.

The store was closed now, though, so Jaime would be home soon unless the problem was a whole lot bigger than Jaime'd led Srikkanth to believe.

The door opened and Jaime trudged in, his shoulders drooping, his head bowed.

"Hey," Srikkanth said softly, not wanting to startle Jaime. "You all right?"

Jaime did his best to summon a smile, but Srikkanth could see the effort it cost him. "Yeah, just tired. I had to fire somebody today because I suspected him of stealing from the store. I hate letting people go under any circumstances, but that was worse than usual."

Srikkanth winced. "Did you have to call the police?"

Jaime nodded. "They took him in for questioning because they didn't have enough proof to charge him yet, but either way, I had to deal with it."

Srikkanth took Jaime's coat from his hands, hanging it on the coat rack near the door and pulling the other man into his arms. "Are you hungry? The curry and rice are ready. I just have to stick them in the microwave for a few minutes."

"I'll get something in a few minutes," Jaime said. "What I'd really like is a stiff drink."

"We don't have any hard liquor, but I think there are a few beers left if you want one of those," Srikkanth offered. "And it's no problem to heat things up for you. Come in the kitchen and have a seat. You've been taking such good care of me. Let me take care of you tonight."

Jaime followed Srikkanth into the kitchen, not voicing a protest. Honestly, he needed it, so tired he wasn't sure he could heat up his own meal. He smiled more genuinely at Srikkanth when his boyfriend brought him a beer. His eyes tracked Srikkanth lazily as he moved around the kitchen, getting out bowls and spooning food into them. "Not that much," Jaime protested. "I'm hungry, yeah, but I'll never eat all that."

"Good," Srikkanth laughed, "because that's supposed to be for both of us. I might be a little put out if you ate my dinner too."

"I told you not to wait to eat," Jaime scolded.

"And I told you to let me take care of you," Srikkanth retorted, putting their dinner in the microwave and coming over to kiss Jaime. "If I'd decided I couldn't wait any longer, I'd have eaten, but I wanted to wait for you. I like eating dinner with you, even if we eat at"—he glanced at the clock—"ten o'clock some nights."

Jaime's smile grew bigger. "Okay, fine. You win. I won't nag anymore."

Srikkanth kissed Jaime again, lingering this time, hoping his attentions would ease some of the tension he could still see on Jaime's face. The microwave dinged to let them know the food was hot, but Srikkanth didn't move right away, preferring to take a moment longer with Jaime. When the other man sighed and relaxed, Srikkanth straightened up. "Do you want paratha? It wouldn't take but another minute to heat it up."

Jaime shook his head. "Not with the rice. Too much starch."

"Okay," Srikkanth said, getting a fork out for Jaime as he went to the microwave and carried the bowls to the table. "Enjoy."

Jaime filled his plate, passing the bowls to Srikkanth when he was done. He had learned to use the various Indian breads as an eating utensil, but he hadn't quite mastered the art of eating rice and curry with his fingers. More ended up back on his plate or in his lap than in his mouth. Srikkanth made it look easy, though, scooping the rice and vegetables into a little ball and into his mouth with practiced ease. It made Jaime want to lean over and lick the long fingers clean. He pushed the thought aside with the first bite, but it came back with a vengeance when Srikkanth smiled just as he pushed a second bite between his even white teeth.

Scooting his chair closer, Jaime reached out and captured Srikkanth's wrist, pulling the sauce-covered fingers to his mouth and sucking them clean.

"Not enough curry on your plate?" Srikkanth husked.

Jaime shook his head. "It just tastes better off your fingers than off my fork."

Srikkanth moaned softly, withdrawing his hand so he could gather another bite, offering it to Jaime along with his fingers. Jaime's lips parted, evoking all sorts of salacious thoughts in Srikkanth's mind as the rice disappeared and Jaime's tongue swiped over his hand.

"More?" Srikkanth asked, voice cracking.

Jaime smiled. "What do you think?"

Not needing more encouragement, Srikkanth offered another mouthful, eyes closing as his cock twitched at the lascivious way Jaime licked his fingers each time. He shifted in his chair, trying to find a more comfortable position, but it didn't do any good with Jaime apparently determined to drive him out of his mind.

"You eat some too," Jaime reminded him when Srikkanth presented every bite to him.

"I like feeding you more."

Jaime's grin widened. "Yeah, but you'll need your strength for later."

"That sounds promising," Srikkanth grinned, popping the next bite in his mouth before offering more to Jaime. If two bites went in Jaime's mouth for every one that Srikkanth ate, Jaime figured it was a better percentage than before.

When they finished eating, Srikkanth started toward the sink, but Jaime caught his hand. "I'll get them in the morning. I don't have to be in until one since I stayed late tonight. Come to bed, Sri."

Srikkanth set the plates on the counter and turned back to Jaime. His eyes glittered with desire, hot and potent, promising all manner of carnal delights if Srikkanth would simply reach out and take them. Turning back to the sink momentarily, he washed his hands, taking extra care to make sure all trace of spices were gone from his hands. He most definitely did not want the oils from the chilies to burn Jaime in sensitive places, and he hoped the look on Jaime's face meant he'd be getting his hands on such places tonight. Assured he wouldn't hurt his boyfriend inadvertently, Srikkanth walked to Jaime's side. "So what's this about bed?"

Jaime laughed and pulled Srikkanth into his arms. "When did Sophie last eat? I'd rather not be interrupted if we can help it."

"About ten minutes before you got home," Srikkanth assured him. "We should have at least an hour until she wakes up. Probably longer."

"Perfect," Jaime purred, taking Srikkanth's hand and leading him toward the downstairs bedroom. "This way we don't have to worry about making too much noise and waking her up."

Srikkanth grinned. "Are we going to be making noise?"

"I certainly hope so! After your display at dinner, I want to know what else your hands are good at besides feeding me."

Srikkanth's stomach tightened with desire. "I think I can oblige."

They tumbled into Jaime's room, crowding each other in their hurry to get inside and undressed. Srikkanth's sweats landed on the floor in a heap. He took a little more care with Jaime's shirt and tie, not wanting to ruin them, but his patience was wearing thin by the time he reached his boyfriend's belt. "Help me here?" he said tartly. "The sooner you get rid of these, the sooner I can show you what else I can do with my hands."

Jaime took a step back and dropped his pants and underwear in one smooth motion, leaving him completely bare standing in the dim room. Srikkanth pounced, needing to touch. They'd slept together the last few nights, but this was the first time he'd had permission, much less an invitation, to touch beyond kissing and a few simple caresses. One hand tangled in Jaime's hair as the other slid around his hip to grab one firm butt cheek, squeezing experimentally. Jaime moaned into the kiss Srikkanth bestowed on him as Srikkanth stroked over the tensile strength of his boyfriend's body, learning the feel of smooth skin beneath his hand. He could imagine getting very addicted to the feeling very quickly.

Deciding he wanted to see more than the light from the other room allowed, Srikkanth flipped on the overhead light, revealing Jaime fully to his gaze. He had the golden skin and dark hair so typical of his Hispanic origin, but Srikkanth knew that already. He was far more interested in the features that made Jaime unique: the curve of his lips as he smiled, the arch of his eyebrows as he stood patiently beneath Srikkanth's examination.

The way his cock jumped beneath Srikkanth's gaze as if he'd touched it.

Jaime was gorgeous, his body lean and hard with muscle, not overly bulky but definitely ripped. Srikkanth could practically feel the heat radiating from Jaime's body, tempting him to step closer and touch the bounty before his eyes.

"About time," Jaime teased when Srikkanth finally moved. "I was beginning to think you'd changed your mind."

"Not likely," Srikkanth retorted. "Not when I've been wanting to touch you all week."

"You've been touching me," Jaime reminded him.

"Not like this," Srikkanth retorted, trailing his fingers over Jaime's cock.

"Fuck, don't tease!"

"I'm not teasing," Srikkanth promised, guiding Jaime back toward the bed. "I'll take care of you."

Jaime lay back, body spread out for Srikkanth's exploration. He had a passing thought for modesty, but the lust glittering in Srikkanth's eyes kept him where he was as Sri climbed onto the bed next to him, sitting on his heels as his fingers started wandering. They traced a meandering path over Jaime's upper body, outlining his chest muscles, circling his aureoles, following the line of his ribs down until they could dip into his navel and brush over his belly. Unable to stop himself, Jaime lifted his hips, straining to bring his erection into contact with Srikkanth's hand.

The movement elicited a chuckle and a kiss from Sri as his hand stroked down the hard length, beginning to caress in earnest. Jaime bucked up into his touch, bringing a smile to Srikkanth's lips as he savored the feeling of hot, hard flesh in his hand. Pulling back so he could sit up and watch Jaime's reactions, he slid his other hand between his boyfriend's legs, finding the heavy sac and cradling it gently, his fingers beginning to manipulate the nodules within. Jaime gasped and parted his legs more, an invitation Srikkanth saw no point in refusing. He cupped Jaime's balls more firmly, working them to the same rhythm as his other hand on Jaime's cock. Before long, his boyfriend was undulating on the bed, begging for more, for release, for anything Srikkanth would give him.

Srikkanth was tempted to draw out their encounter, but his own body was demanding attention now. Since he doubted Jaime would agree to let Srikkanth fuck him, that meant getting Jaime off so he could take care of Srikkanth's needs. Soon.

Increasing the speed of his strokes over the hard shaft, Srikkanth bent his head and kissed his boyfriend again. "Come on, Jaime," he urged. "Show me how good it feels."

"Too good," Jaime gasped. "Can't wait much longer."

"Don't," Srikkanth insisted. "Come all over my hand."

The words were all the encouragement Jaime needed, his cock disgorging its load over his belly and Srikkanth's fist. Srikkanth kept stroking through the aftershocks until Jaime whimpered and stilled his wrist. "Too much," he moaned.

Leaning down for another kiss, Srikkanth let his hand settle on Jaime's hip, keeping the contact without doing anything else to arouse his lover.

He smiled.

His lover.

It had been awhile since he'd had a steady boyfriend, much less someone he wanted to consider a lover. Looking down at Jaime, he wondered if he'd ever want anyone else.

"What can I do for you now?" Jaime asked, pushing up on one elbow as awareness returned post-orgasm.

Srikkanth hesitated, not sure how Jaime would feel about him voicing his desires. "You could just—"

"I don't want to 'just' anything," Jaime interrupted. "Tell me what you want."

Srikkanth gulped. "Your mouth," he whispered. "I sat there at dinner watching your lips and imagining...."

He didn't finish the sentence, but he didn't have to. Jaime rose up on one elbow and pushed him onto the bed, tugging the elastic of his underwear down over the bulge at his groin. Without waiting for encouragement or permission, Jaime lowered his head and licked a stripe from base to tip. Srikkanth collapsed the rest of the way onto the bed, moaning in delight at the wet heat that suddenly enveloped the tip of his cock.

Jaime grinned up at him. "I think you like that."

Srikkanth nodded helplessly, amazed at the power of the fantasy made real. Jaime's plump lips stretched beautifully around the tip of Sri's cock, leaving Srikkanth gasping for breath as they slid down the shaft. He groaned Jaime's name, not entirely sure what he wanted. Only that he didn't want it to stop.

Fortunately, Jaime seemed to know exactly how to interpret the sound, his mouth increasing its suction until Srikkanth thrust up into the welcoming cavern, the tip of his cock bumping the back of Jaime's throat. Jaime pulled back for a moment, adjusting the angle before sinking down again and taking Srikkanth's full length into his throat.

Srikkanth moaned loudly, glad Jaime had insisted they come in here rather than going upstairs to his room where he'd be constantly worried about waking Sophie. Jaime's mouth was far too talented not to praise effusively.

"So good," he husked. "Feels even better than I'd imagined."

Jaime released the flesh in his mouth with a loud pop. "And just how long have you been imagining it?"

Srikkanth felt his cheeks burn. "Longer than I should've been."

Jaime grinned, stroking his hand over Srikkanth's balls. "That makes two of us."

Before Srikkanth could come up with a reply to that, Jaime had lowered his head again and resumed his attentions, leaving Srikkanth incapable of doing anything more than thrashing on the bed and coming hard.

Jaime swallowed every drop, licking and sucking until Srikkanth had nothing left to give. The stimulation finally became too much on his sensitive flesh, and he pulled away. Jaime moved up next to him, pulling him close.

"We can't fall asleep down here," Srikkanth warned. "We won't hear Sophie."

"We won't fall asleep," Jaime promised. "Just let me hold you for a few minutes and then we'll go upstairs and sleep in your bed so we can hear our little girl if she needs us."

CHAPTER TWELVE

THE knock on the door surprised Srikkanth, but he juggled Sophie so he could answer the door. A woman he didn't know stood on his doorstep, flanked by a man in a suit and a police officer. "Mr. Bhattacharya?"

"Yes," Srikkanth replied warily.

"My name is Ellen Fitz. I'm with Child Protective Services. This is Mr. Peters of the crisis intervention team and Officer Matthews. Can we go inside to talk? It's a little chilly here on the doorstep."

Srikkanth felt his stomach clench even as he stepped back instinctively, allowing the three people access to the house. "Is there a problem?"

"That's what we're here to find out," she explained, though it was really no explanation at all as far as Srikkanth was concerned. "We received a call alleging there was a child in danger here, so we have to check it out. Are you alone in the house?"

"In danger?" Srikkanth parroted. "But the only child here is Sophie. How is she in danger?"

"The report alleged she was in danger from you," Ms. Fitz explained. "You didn't answer my question, Mr. Bhattacharya. Are you alone in the house?"

"Y-yes," Srikkanth stuttered, eyes flying from one stern face to the next. "But I would never do anything to hurt Sophie," Srikkanth insisted. "I love her."

"I'm sure you do," Ms. Fitz allowed, "but people hurt their loved ones every day. I'll need to check her to make sure she's not hurt in any way."

Automatically, Srikkanth cradled her closer to his chest, not wanting to turn her over, but the police officer took a step forward, and Srikkanth realized he didn't have any choice in the matter. Trying to tell himself he hadn't done anything wrong and that they wouldn't find anything to substantiate their claim, he reluctantly handed his daughter to the social worker.

"Support her head," he directed. "She's getting better about holding it up, but she doesn't always keep it steady when she's being moved as opposed to moving herself."

Ms. Fitz reached for Sophie confidently, so Srikkanth fell silent, heart aching a little when she started crying at the unfamiliar face above her. Ms. Fitz didn't seem bothered by the sound, opening the zipper on Sophie's pajamas and examining her carefully.

Sophie cried a little louder when cold fingers pulled her diaper away and prodded her skin. Srikkanth bit his lip to keep from grabbing her back from the social worker, only the police officer still hovering protectively enough to stop him.

"She looks in good health," Ms. Fitz said finally, handing Sophie to the man in the suit. "Mr. Peters will hold her until we're finished with our conversation." Srikkanth's desire to grab Sophie back and run grew, but his stomach roiled as he realized they held all the cards at the moment.

"Of course she's in good health," Srikkanth snapped, his anxiety shortening his words. "I know enough to feed her and keep her diaper changed, and anything I don't know, Jaime tells me."

"Who is Jaime?"

"My partner, Jaime Frias. He's at work right now. Do I need to call him?" Srikkanth almost hoped she said yes so he would have Jaime's support as he dealt with the social worker and her accusations. Jaime would know how to deal with them, would be able to keep his cool and deflect their concerns with his easy smile and experienced confidence.

"That isn't necessary at the moment," she replied. "If I decide I need to speak with him, I'll get his number. Officer Matthews is going to check the rest of the house while Mr. Peters and I finish talking to you. Is Sophie a fussy baby?"

"Not usually," Srikkanth replied, his eyes tracking the officer's movements as he went into the kitchen and from there into Jaime's room. He could hear the cop opening doors and drawers, and his sense of violation grew with each noise. "Occasionally she'll get a bit of colic, but it doesn't last very long."

"How do you handle it when she does have colic?"

"I walk her or rock her until she wears herself out and falls asleep," Srikkanth answered, not liking where the questions were leading. They were searching for fault, anything they could find to give them an excuse to take Sophie from him.

"And if that doesn't work?"

Srikkanth smiled despite the tension growing inside him at the thought of Jaime cradling Sophie so tenderly, even when she'd been crying for hours. "If I can't get her calmed down, I give her to Jaime. He can always get her to settle."

"Have you ever shaken her?"

"No!" Srikkanth exclaimed, his anger returning as his sense of being hounded increased again. "I'd never do that to her. I don't want to hurt her neck."

"Are you her primary caregiver?"

"Yes. I work from home most days. She stays with Jaime on Mondays when I'm in the office," Srikkanth explained. "I don't mean to be rude, Ms. Fitz, but I don't really understand why you're here. I mean, other than one ear infection, Sophie is a perfectly healthy, happy baby."

"I'm here because someone called Child Protective Services to report that she was being abused," Ms. Fitz repeated. The police officer came out of Jaime's room through the bathroom and started up the stairs. Srikkanth told himself the sooner he let the man do his job, the sooner he'd be able to shut the door behind them once and for all, but that didn't make it any easier to picture the man pawing through Sophie's things, searching his room for anything that might be a danger to her.

"But who?" Srikkanth demanded. "I was as ignorant as any first-time parent when Sophie came home from the hospital, but that doesn't make me abusive."

"What about Sophie's mother?" Ms. Fitz inquired. "You've mentioned Mr. Frias several times, but not her mother."

"Jill died in childbirth," Srikkanth replied flatly. "Sophie came home with me when she was four days old. Jill and I weren't a couple, if that's your next question. She was a good friend, but not a girlfriend."

"And Mr. Frias?" the social worker asked, glancing down at her notes.

"Jaime has been my housemate since I bought the condo three years ago," Srikkanth said. "When I found out about Jill, he offered to help me take care of Sophie since I didn't know what I was doing."

"You referred to him as your partner," Ms. Fitz reminded him. "I realize this is an invasion of your privacy, Mr. Bhattacharya, but I need you to be honest with me so I can deal with the situation appropriately and not have to bother you again if it isn't warranted."

"I don't see how my personal life matters," Srikkanth defended himself. "Sophie isn't being abused!"

"That's what everyone I visit says," Ms. Fitz told him sadly. The police officer came back downstairs and shook his head. "However, we haven't found anything for the moment to substantiate the claim. Sophie is, as you said, a healthy baby, and

Officer Matthews hasn't found any worrisome conditions in the house, so we'll be going now."

"Can you at least tell me who reported us?" Srikkanth asked, taking Sophie back gratefully from Mr. Peters.

"No, that's confidential information," Ms. Fitz replied. "We will, however, take any future reports from the same source with a grain of salt. When a first report comes in, we have to take it seriously. This report was obviously unfounded, though, so we'll keep that in mind should we get another call."

"They did this because Jaime and I are gay, didn't they?" Srikkanth said bitterly.

"That isn't a question I can answer," Ms. Fitz demurred. "Nor is that the business of my office. As long as Sophie is healthy, which she obviously is, we aren't concerned about your private life."

"I don't like that someone can disrupt our lives with a phone call," Srikkanth admitted.

"I understand," Ms. Fitz replied. "I really do. Unfortunately, it works that way because people have to feel like they can report abuse if they see it. We miss enough kids as it is."

"And so you spent an hour or more today driving here to investigate a false report."

Ms. Fitz shrugged. "It's what I do. The system isn't perfect, but I do believe in it because it does help kids. Sophie doesn't need my help, but if she had, she'd have gotten it."

"Sophie has everything she needs with her two dads," Srikkanth insisted, cradling Sophie more tightly against him, relieved that her cries had subsided to little whimpers now that she was back in his arms. "Jaime and I are perfectly capable of taking care of her."

"I believe you are. I'll be going now," Ms. Fitz said. "Enjoy the rest of your day."

Srikkanth showed her out, standing on the steps as the three walked down the sidewalk.

"I suspected this was a false alarm," he overheard Ms. Fitz say as they neared the car. "With the amount of anti-gay nonsense the caller was spouting, I almost dismissed it out of hand, but I couldn't take that risk."

"You did the right thing," Mr. Peters insisted. "As you said, she's healthy, so we won't need to come back, but you couldn't have known that from the call."

Head pounding with a combination of revulsion and anger, Srikkanth backed inside, not waiting to hear if they said anymore. He'd heard more than enough. Knowing nothing else would calm him down, he carried Sophie upstairs to the nursery. She had returned to her generally sunny state, but he needed the reassurance of sitting with her in his arms and rocking her. They weren't going to take his baby! He didn't care what he had to do. Sophie was his daughter, and he loved her. Whoever had made the phone call could rot in hell for all he cared.

He didn't realize his grip had tightened or that he was muttering under his breath until Sophie squirmed in his arms, protesting the strength of his hold on her. "I'm sorry, *betti*," he whispered, bending to kiss her forehead. "I didn't mean to squeeze you so hard. I just love you so much and don't want anything to happen to you or to our family. I don't know what we're going to do, but we'll figure something out. I promise Jaime and I will take care of you. You just have to trust us and let us do what needs to be done."

Sophie cooed up at her adored father, sensing his mood as babies were wont to do.

He couldn't help smiling down at her. She brightened even the darkest moments.

A quick glance at the clock revealed he'd missed her usual feeding time. Not by much, but she'd be getting hungry soon. "Let's go make a bottle for you," he suggested, rising and starting back downstairs. "We'll get you fed and down for your nap and then Daddy will get some work done while you're resting. And when you wake up, Jaime should be home. You'll be glad to see him, won't you? I know I will be."

Sophie cooed again.

Srikkanth laughed despite the tension of the morning, much of it slipping away now that the social worker had gone. He'd talk to Jaime that evening and see what he thought.

JAIME got home in time to start making dinner, surprised to find Srikkanth simply sitting on the couch holding Sophie.

"Hey, Sri," he said as he came in. "You all right?"

Srikkanth shook his head. "Not really. We had a visit today from Child Protective Services. Someone reported us for child abuse."

"On what grounds?" Jaime demanded, outrage filling him at the idea that someone would suggest such a thing about Srikkanth and at the fact that his boyfriend had dealt with it alone.

"On the grounds that I'm gay," Srikkanth said bluntly. "Oh, they didn't say that, I'm sure, but I overheard the social worker tell her colleague that they spouted some anti-gay bullshit—sorry, Sophie—along with the report of abuse. The team didn't find anything, of course, but that doesn't make it less stressful."

"A team?" Jaime repeated, sitting down next to Srikkanth and enfolding him in a tender embrace. "You should have called me. I'd have come home."

"I know," Srikkanth said, lifting his head and meeting Jaime's doubting eyes. "I really do know, but there wasn't anything you could've done. It's not like the social worker actually tried to take Sophie from us. She checked her out, saw she was healthy, no bruises, well fed, happy, and asked a bunch of questions."

It hadn't been anywhere near that simple, Jaime suspected. "What aren't you telling me? You said the team. Who else was here besides the social worker?"

"A crisis team member and a cop," Srikkanth said with a shudder. "The crisis team member didn't do much but hold Sophie the whole time, but the cop searched the house. God, Jaime, the whole time I was sitting there trying to answer their questions, not knowing what they were trying to prove, I could hear the officer going through the house, opening doors and drawers and.... I feel like I should scrub the house from top to bottom, except that wouldn't get the memories out of my head."

"And you've been sitting here brooding about it ever since," Jaime surmised, hearing the desolation in Srikkanth's voice. "Let's go out. We can go to a restaurant for dinner. Even if it's just Perkins. You'll feel better if you get out of the house for a bit."

Srikkanth shook his head automatically. "I think we should keep a low profile for a bit. Maybe whoever did this will think CPS took Sophie if they don't see us with her for awhile. At the very least, out of sight is out of mind."

Jaime frowned, but he could understand Srikkanth's hunker down mentality. "Okay, if you really don't want to go out, I'll get Chinese. It's fast and good and I won't have to cook. I can give you all my attention instead."

Srikkanth nodded, but his free arm snaked around Jaime's waist, holding him close. "In a few minutes, okay? Don't go yet."

Jaime pulled Srikkanth closer, urging him to rest his head on Jaime's shoulder. "I'm not going anywhere," he promised. "You and Sophie are stuck with me."

Srikkanth smiled. "That's the best thing I've heard all day."

Jaime kissed Srikkanth's temple and simply sat there holding him. Inwardly, he seethed, though, trying to figure out who among their neighbors could have made such a pernicious call. The visit had destroyed Srikkanth's sense of security in his own home, and

Jaime hated that. Having a refuge was so important, and that had been stolen from Srikkanth today with one lie-filled phone call. Jaime didn't know how to restore it, but he knew he'd try. If it meant scrubbing the house from top to bottom, he'd do it. If it meant redoing all the rooms, he'd work overtime to find the money. If it meant moving somewhere else, he'd call a realtor tomorrow.

Softly humming his grandmother's favorite lullaby, he let Srikkanth go long enough to reach for Sophie. "She's asleep," he murmured. "Let me put her in her bed."

"I haven't been able to put her down all afternoon," Srikkanth admitted hoarsely. "It's like if I'm not holding her, I'm afraid they'll take her."

"Nobody's trying to take her," Jaime reassured him. "The social worker left and she's still here with you. She's safe and so are you. If you want to keep her where you can see her, I'll bring the bouncer in here, but you need a break too. You're obviously worn out. Let me get her settled and then we can lie together on the couch and make out. How does that sound?"

"Pretty damn perfect," Srikkanth replied with a sigh, letting Jaime take Sophie. His arms felt painfully empty without her warm weight, but he reminded himself Sophie was as safe with Jaime as she was with him and they were only going to the other room and back. If he wanted to, he could stand up and watch their progress the entire time. That required more energy than he had at the moment, though, so he let his head fall against the back of the couch and listened for Jaime's footsteps instead. He could track their progress that way. The same way he'd tracked the policeman through the house. He pushed aside that thought, clinging to Jaime's reminder that Sophie was still here with them and the crisis team had left.

The reassuring tread returned, and Srikkanth opened his eyes to watch Jaime settle Sophie into her bouncer, fastening the seatbelt so she couldn't slide out and turning on the vibrations to soothe her if she stirred. Her eyelids didn't even flutter as he tucked a blanket around her and joined Srikkanth on the couch again. "There, she's all settled. Now let me take care of you."

Srikkanth moved into Jaime's arms, eager for the comfort they would provide. He hated feeling helpless, but he didn't know how to fight this battle. He'd never needed to before. With a sigh, he settled in the crook of Jaime's arm, his head on Jaime's shoulder as his lover pulled the afghan from the back of the couch and spread it over them. Cocooned in warmth and the safety of Jaime's embrace, Srikkanth felt the fear slowly fading from his heart. With Jaime holding him, he could do anything. Even face down the people who wanted to take Sophie away from him because of his sexuality. He snorted softly.

"What?" Jaime asked.

"I was just thinking that the very thing that will give me the strength to fight these bastards is the reason they're doing this in the first place," Srikkanth explained. "The weapon they think to use against me is my greatest ally."

Jaime smiled. "They won't beat us. Social services can't take Sophie because we're gay. As long as we take good care of her, all the bastards can do is make life difficult. They can't win."

"Maybe not," Srikkanth agreed, "but I think I won't take Sophie to the park again right away. I don't know where the caller saw us, but the less they see of us for awhile the better."

Jaime wasn't sure that was the right approach, but he simply held Srikkanth tighter. "Just remember that you don't have to face this, or anything, alone. Even if all you do is call me after the fact to let me know what's happening."

"I know that," Srikkanth mumbled. "I told the social worker you were my partner. There just wasn't anything you could do."

The word "partner" struck Jaime right in the breastbone. Not boyfriend. Not roommate. Not even lover. Partner. Now if Srikkanth would just act like he believed it.

CHAPTER THIRTEEN

"IT'S a beautiful day," Jaime said when he got home from work one day about two weeks later. "We should take Sophie to the park."

Srikkanth had steadfastly refused to take Sophie anywhere since the social worker's visit, and Jaime was getting tired of it. He understood the impulse, but he felt like they were letting their detractor win.

"Not today," Srikkanth said with a shake of his head. "Maybe another day."

"Yes, but the sun is shining today, and it's supposed to rain the rest of the week. Come on, Sri. Let's go for a walk," Jaime cajoled, resting his head on Srikkanth's shoulder and putting his arms around his boyfriend's waist.

Srikkanth tensed in his arms, drawing a sigh from Jaime's throat. He silently cursed whichever of their neighbors had called the social worker. Not only was Srikkanth worried about taking Sophie outside, but he'd also started resisting signs of affection when Sophie was in the same room. "I said not today," Srikkanth repeated, pulling away.

"Do you mind if I take her then?" Jaime asked. "I really think it would do her some good to get some fresh air."

"So now you think I'm not taking good care of her either?" Srikkanth demanded.

"That's not at all what I meant," Jaime said evenly, struggling to keep a hold of his temper. "I simply think we'd all enjoy a walk."

"I wouldn't," Srikkanth said stubbornly, "and I don't want her to go out either. Seeing her with you would be even worse than seeing her with me. At least I'm her father."

"Oh, and I'm just some stranger?" Jaime demanded. "Some random hookup who doesn't care anything about either of you? Well fuck that. You're letting them win, Srikkanth. Every time you refuse to do something harmless like going for a walk because someone might see and disapprove, you're giving them that much more power over you. Is that the way you want to raise your daughter? Afraid to go outside? Ashamed of her father because he prefers men to women?"

"Of course not!" Srikkanth retorted. "That doesn't mean I should expose her needlessly to other people's intolerance."

"Then take her to the park," Jaime insisted. "Be proud of her and of yourself."

"I can't," Srikkanth said, his voice defeated.

"Are you really going to let them drive you back into the closet?" Jaime asked slowly.

"That's not what I'm doing. I'm protecting Sophie. You weren't here. You don't know what it was like!"

Jaime shook his head. "You're crawling back in the closet with your tail between your legs and you're trying to drag me with you. I can't control what you do, but I won't do it. I'm going for a walk."

Not even bothering to change his shoes, Jaime walked back out the door, slamming it behind him in frustration. He'd tried so hard to be supportive, to understand what Srikkanth was suffering because of one person's intolerance, but he'd fought the battle of coming out once, dealing with his relatively conservative family and their initially horrified reactions. He was proud of who he was, proud of the life he'd built for himself. Hiding what he felt for Srikkanth and Sophie, denying themselves a normal life, felt wrong, like it invalidated all those earlier struggles.

His feet took him to the park down the street where he and Srikkanth had gone on their first "date." He sank onto the bench, his head in his hands as he tried to see a way forward. He was irrevocably in love with Sophie. Losing her now would be like losing his own child, something he couldn't even imagine. He couldn't stay with someone who was ashamed of him, though. However much he wanted to be a part of Sophie's life, he didn't want to live in fear of someone finding out about them. He didn't think Srikkanth actually wanted that lifestyle either, but it was the one he was living at the moment, and Jaime couldn't be a part of that.

That thought hurt nearly as much as the thought of saying goodbye to Sophie. He and Srikkanth had been friends for years, and the past four months, helping him with Sophie, had been some of the best of his life. His chest ached as he remembered how right it felt to lie in Srikkanth's bed knowing Sophie was sleeping in the next room, to wake together in the morning and rise to face the day as a unit, stronger together than either of them could ever be apart. If they'd never taken that step, if he'd stayed Srikkanth's friend who helped him out with the baby from time to time, it might have been easier to take a step back now, but they'd broken their cardinal rule, and he wasn't just facing losing a daughter he never expected to have. He was facing losing a lover he hadn't known he wanted.

It had only been two weeks since the social worker's visit. He could give Srikkanth more time, see if things got better, if he became less cautious again as the fear faded, but Jaime had no guarantee that would work. Breaking up with Srikkanth would be hard enough now. To allow himself more time to fall in love would only make it worse. If he was going to make the decision to pull back, it had to be now, when he had some hope of keeping his heart intact.

His eyes stung at the thought as he blinked back unexpected tears. When had he fallen so hard? He tried to think back, to pinpoint the moment his emotions changed from supportive friendship to more, but he couldn't put his finger on any single event. Rather than an epiphanous moment, it had been a slow progression, the sense of family once Sophie was part of their lives growing incrementally until the feeling of belonging was too strong to ignore any longer. He couldn't have both, though. He knew himself well enough to know that the argument today would be only the beginning if he let things stay as they were. He'd have that sense of family a little while longer, but his resentment would grow as well until they fought more and more. Sophie deserved better than that. If he left now, she wouldn't be subjected to that, wouldn't even remember him.

Everyone would be better off that way. He knew it, but his heart protested the dual loss. Steeling his resolve, he rose and continued his walk, trying to release the anger and pain so he could explain the situation to Srikkanth as matter-of-factly as possible. He didn't want a big scene. He didn't want to make Srikkanth feel guilty, but this was a line he could not cross and remain true to himself.

When Jaime got home, he let himself inside and looked around for Srikkanth, but the living room and kitchen were empty, only the lamp next to the couch providing any light. His heart clenched as he walked into the kitchen and saw the plate Srikkanth had obviously prepared for him. Reheating his dinner, he ate in silence, feeling the gulf widening with each passing moment. He knew Srikkanth was in the house. His car was in its parking spot, and occasionally Jaime would hear a footstep upstairs, but he didn't call out to let the other man know he was home. He couldn't. If he did, Srikkanth would come downstairs and Jaime would have to explain everything. He knew they needed to talk, but not right now. Not when Jaime's heart was still breaking over the decision he'd made.

Finishing his dinner, he took a deep breath and went into his room on the main floor, locking the door behind him. Another hour passed before he heard Srikkanth come back downstairs, calling his name softly. Jaime wanted to open the door and go to him, but one of two things would happen if he did. Either Srikkanth would reach for him and all Jaime's resolve would crumble, leaving them back in the same situation that led to their fight earlier, or else Srikkanth would try to continue their discussion and Jaime would lose his temper again. Neither option was acceptable, so he stayed where he was, clicking off his light and pretending to be asleep despite the fact that it wasn't even nine o'clock.

SRIKKANTH stared at the closed door helplessly. He could feel the schism between Jaime and himself deepening, but he couldn't bridge the gap by himself. He needed Jaime to meet him halfway, and the closed door didn't invite his visit. Remembering his mother's advice to his sister on the eve of her wedding to never go to bed angry at her husband, Srikkanth called Jaime's name again, trying the door handle.

It was locked.

Defeated, he went back upstairs, not confident enough in his position to try to force the issue more than he'd already done. From Jaime's perspective, Srikkanth had created this mess. Srikkanth got that, but no amount of reasoning would ease his fears. Someone had threatened his baby, his family, and he couldn't simply forget that because his method of protecting them didn't meet with Jaime's approval. It had only taken one phone call to have the police on his doorstep. They hadn't found anything and had left again, but that didn't mean they wouldn't be back if they received another call. Even if they didn't find anything more than they'd found the first time, the repeated trauma of dealing with social services would wear him down and tear him apart.

His empty bed taunted him with his failure, the sheets cold after sleeping next to Jaime's warmth, his fears heightened in the chilling light of Jaime's absence. It might not take an outside force to tear apart his family. If he couldn't find a way to resolve things with Jaime, it could very well be torn apart from the inside. He tossed and turned for an hour, unable to settle. Giving up finally, he wandered into Sophie's room, hoping her presence would soothe him. She was as restless as he was, it seemed, as she tossed in her bed. He picked her up and rocked her gently, memories of all the nights Jaime had come in to help him assailing him as he sat there with her in his arms. He caught himself looking toward the door, expecting to see Jaime there as he'd been so many nights—almost every night since Nathaniel moved out—but the doorway stayed empty, as empty as Srikkanth's bed. The repetitive rocking and the warm weight of Sophie's body in his arms eventually lulled him into a doze despite his emotional turmoil, his head falling forward awkwardly onto his chest. The movement roused him enough for him to stand up carefully, tucking Sophie back into her crib, but he didn't leave the room. Everything was topsy-turvy in his head, and the thought of returning to an empty bed didn't appeal at all. He could go downstairs and try again to force a resolution with Jaime, except that he didn't want it to be forced. He needed Jaime to want this as much as he did. Unfortunately that didn't seem to be the case, and waking him up at well after midnight wouldn't help. With a sigh, he turned toward the day bed, but Jaime had given him that as well and had snuggled with him in it as they fed Sophie. Everywhere he turned, memories lurked. Grumbling a little, he pulled the quilt from the bed and tried to find a comfortable position in the rocking chair.

SRIKKANTH didn't see Jaime the next morning before Jaime left for work. The other man timed his presence in the kitchen so that he was in and out while Srikkanth was changing Sophie's diaper. He left without even saying goodbye to Sophie, a fact that stung far worse than Jaime leaving without saying goodbye to Srikkanth.

Srikkanth got that Jaime was angry with him. He even thought he understood why, although he wasn't ready to simply accede to Jaime's demands, but Sophie hadn't done anything to upset Jaime, yet she, too, was suffering because of their ongoing fight. He could tell she was looking for Jaime, but all he could do was promise her he would come home that night and that he still loved her. He only hoped he wasn't lying.

Jaime came home at his regular time, much to Srikkanth's relief. A part of him he hadn't wanted to acknowledge feared Jaime wouldn't come home at all. Srikkanth got a cool greeting, little more than a perfunctory nod, but Jaime cooed over Sophie, giving Srikkanth the comfort of knowing he had not lied to his daughter. Dinner was a tense affair, neither man speaking to the other, all their conversation directed at Sophie. Srikkanth's stomach got tighter as the meal stretched interminably, the silence making him realize how warm their friendship had always been, even before they'd started something more. To have that torn away hurt far worse than any breakup he'd gone through before. Then again, he'd never started a family with any of his previous boyfriends or had a relationship with a roommate.

He hoped for a chance to talk to Jaime after Sophie went to bed, but while Jaime kissed her goodnight, he didn't follow Srikkanth upstairs as he usually did to help with her bath and bedtime, and when Srikkanth came back downstairs after getting her settled, Jaime had gone out without leaving a note. Srikkanth considered waiting in the living room for him to come home, but he didn't know what time, or even if, Jaime would get home, and he didn't want to seem desperate. Neither one of them had to work the next day, so he'd have time then, and the memory of the locked door stayed with him, a reminder that Jaime didn't want to see him. With a sigh, he climbed back upstairs, trying to get comfortable in his bed. He couldn't spend another night in Sophie's rocking chair. His neck and back had ached all day because of last night. The bed was just as cold and empty as the night before, though, and it took a long time before he finally fell asleep.

He didn't wake up when Jaime came upstairs later that night and stood in the doorway for several minutes before going into the nursery and giving Sophie a bottle. Jaime rocked her for a long time after she'd fallen back asleep, needing the closeness with her since he couldn't have it with her father right now. He'd gone for a run after dinner, needing to release the stress of work and of the impasse with Srikkanth. It had done its job, but it had also given him even more to think about. In the park, he'd encountered another family very much like the one he'd thought he and Srikkanth were creating. The child was older, five or six probably, but that only strengthened Jaime's resolve. He'd actually stopped and approached the couple, introducing himself and asking them about reactions to their family. The men had replied that they did sometimes encounter prejudice still, but that being together, being a family, more than made up for it. They'd taught their son what to say in the face of insults and to be proud of who he was and who his parents were. Jaime had thanked them and continued his run, aching even more for what he knew he and Srikkanth could have if only Srikkanth would let them. Kissing Sophie's forehead one more time, he set her back in her crib and went downstairs, wondering how long he could stand to wait for Srikkanth to come to his senses. He refused to admit that Srikkanth might never change his mind.

THE next morning, Srikkanth received the same cool nod as the day before, nothing in Jaime's demeanor giving away his late night excursion. He missed Srikkanth desperately, but he couldn't be the one to give in, not if he wanted to retain any sense of self-respect. He might be able to live the way Srikkanth wanted for a few weeks, maybe even a month or two, but eventually he'd come to resent him, and the resulting explosion would be far worse than what he was feeling right now. At least at the moment, he still had Sophie. He wanted that to continue, but he couldn't do what Srikkanth asked. Not in any permanent fashion. He couldn't force Srikkanth to change his mind, though, which meant waiting until Srikkanth was ready to change his mind and hoping against hope that it wouldn't be too long. After the past three months, he didn't know if he could go back to just being a roommate. If he moved out, though, he'd lose his connection to Sophie entirely.

Trying not to let his longing show too strongly on his face, he offered to watch Sophie for a few hours if Srikkanth had any errands he needed to run. "Since you aren't going out with her while I'm gone."

Srikkanth flinched at the comment, making Jaime feel bad, but he didn't apologize. Srikkanth had to see how ridiculous he was acting. "I do need to go to the grocery," Srikkanth agreed. "Are you sure you don't mind watching her?"

"When have I ever minded watching her?" Jaime asked acerbically, trying not to be offended that Srikkanth would think their change in relationship would affect his relationship with Sophie. "She isn't the one who made me angry."

"About that—"

"You know where I stand," Jaime interrupted, not wanting to get into the discussion again. "Go get your groceries and whatever else you need. Sophie and I will be fine here while you're gone."

He didn't give Srikkanth the chance to continue the conversation. He simply picked Sophie up and went to his room, shutting the door behind him to end the discussion.

When he heard the door to the condo shut behind Srikkanth, he carried Sophie back into the living room, picking up some of her toys and settling with her on the floor. He put her down on her blanket and lay down beside her, dangling her favorite rattle in front of her. She smiled and cooed and reached for it, her little arms flailing as she tried to make her fingers and eyes work together. "How stubborn is your daddy going to be?" he asked her after a moment.

She blinked at him with her owlishly big eyes.

"How long is he going to pretend he wants to live like this, with us hardly talking and you caught in the middle?" Jaime went on. "You have to know I don't want it this way. I want it the way things were before the social worker came to visit, before one person's prejudice scared your father into hiding. I can't make him change, though, so we'll have to be patient. No matter what happens, I want you to remember that I love you."

SRIKKANTH came home to the most beautiful sight he could've imagined. Instinctively, he started toward Jaime and Sophie, wanting to join them, to be part of the perfect tableau, but the moment Jaime heard him, he stood up and ceded his place to Srikkanth. "Jaime—"

"Thank you for letting me watch her," Jaime interrupted, not letting Srikkanth continue. He knew Srikkanth wanted him to stay, but he couldn't do it. He couldn't play house with Srikkanth and Sophie here if Srikkanth wasn't willing to take that relationship outside the walls of their condo.

"You don't have to leave," Srikkanth persisted.

Jaime smiled sadly. "Yes, I do. I won't pretend, Sri. I can't. I'm sorry."

CHAPTER FOURTEEN

MONDAY had to be the longest day of the week, Srikkanth decided as he drove home from work. He'd even managed to get away early, and it had still felt never-ending. With a relieved sigh, he pulled into the parking lot and walked up the steps, listening for the sound of Jaime's voice and Sophie's laughter. He didn't want to disturb his daughter if she was asleep.

Silence greeted him as he opened the door. He slipped upstairs to peek into Sophie's room, but her crib was empty. Frowning, he set down his briefcase and went back downstairs to check Jaime's room. It was empty as well.

His heart seized. He told himself Jaime had simply taken Sophie for a walk, but that didn't slow his pulse as he ran to the window. Jaime's car was in the parking lot, but that merely meant he was on foot or that someone else had driven him. Visions of the social worker and police returning and taking both Sophie and Jaime away tormented him as he grabbed his cell phone and dialed Jaime's number. The phone rang in the downstairs bedroom. Stomach twisting tighter at the thought that wherever Jaime was, he didn't have his phone, Srikkanth dug his keys back out of his pocket. He'd drive around the neighborhood a bit to see if he could find them, and then if not, he'd start making phone calls. He didn't have the slightest idea where to start with the calls, but he'd figure it out.

Srikkanth drove around the condo complex first, thinking Jaime might have gone out to get some fresh air, but he didn't find them. Leaving the gated parking lot, he circled the neighborhood in ever-increasing circles, driving far more slowly than he usually would as he searched for his missing family.

He found them about twenty minutes later—the longest twenty minutes of his life—in the nearby park. Jaime held Sophie as he sat on a bench with another man while a third man played catch with a school-aged boy. Srikkanth's stomach sank with miserable jealousy until the boy ran up to the man on the bench, dragging the pitcher behind him, and gave the seated one a hug. The pitcher bent as well, giving a quick kiss to his partner. Srikkanth let out the breath he hadn't known he was holding, his heart pounding now for a different reason.

Leaving Sophie and Jaime to their walk, he drove slowly back home, his thoughts all awhirl.

Sitting down at the kitchen table, he leaned his chin on his hands and tried to make everything fit back into place.

It didn't.

It couldn't because he had an extra piece now, one he hadn't expected, hadn't identified until now, and it changed everything. He'd almost gotten used to thinking of himself and Sophie as a unit, of planning for a future with them together. He still wanted that, but seeing Jaime talking to the man in the park had driven home one other realization.

He was in love with Jaime.

And that changed everything.

With that immutable fact in mind, he found himself reconsidering his position. Jaime had made his expectations very clear. Srikkanth didn't know if his roommate—no, his lover. Srikkanth was determined to win him back—felt the same way Srikkanth did, but if he didn't find a way to compromise, he wouldn't have a chance at all. That meant facing his fears and finding a way to keep them under control even if he couldn't completely let them go.

He'd dealt with prejudice before, both because of his ethnicity and because of his sexuality. He'd learned to deal with it for himself, either by ignoring it or by fighting it, but this time it threatened Sophie, and his protective instincts had kicked in, causing him to retreat in an effort to protect his child. He didn't think any parent would question that instinctive reaction, but Jaime was right as well. They couldn't live that way. Sophie needed to go out, to be around other people. She needed to grow up free of fear and secure in the belief that her parents were as proud of themselves as they were of her. He prayed he hadn't lost his chance with Jaime and that he'd find a way to convince Jaime he wanted a life together for the three of them.

When Jaime and Sophie came home half an hour later, he hadn't moved from his spot.

"You're home early," Jaime commented slowly, not sure how Srikkanth would react to the fact that he'd taken Sophie out for a walk.

"I missed you," Srikkanth said by way of explanation. "Both of you."

"Sri—"

"No, don't interrupt me this time," Srikkanth insisted. "I'm sorry. I let fear get in the way of what was important, and that wasn't fair to you or to Sophie."

Jaime nodded slowly, heart beating a little faster at Srikkanth's words. "Let's eat dinner and put Sophie to bed and then we'll talk, all right?"

"As long as you don't run away from me again," Srikkanth pressed. "You've run away every time I've tried to talk to you for the last two days."

"We'll talk after dinner," Jaime repeated, not wanting to start this now. It wouldn't be a short or easy conversation, he suspected, and he'd rather wait to have it until they could talk uninterrupted for as long as they needed to.

Srikkanth subsided and Jaime let it go, turning his attention to Sophie as they fixed dinner and ate. He was tempted to follow Srikkanth upstairs for Sophie's bath, but they hadn't resolved anything between them yet, and he didn't want to presume. If the conversation went the way he hoped, he'd be back up there with them soon, maybe even tonight. If not…. As much as he didn't want to think about the "if not," he knew he had to accept that possibility and protect himself from the hurt as much as he could. He kissed her forehead tenderly and told her he loved her before Srikkanth took her upstairs. For now, that would have to be enough.

Srikkanth came back downstairs an hour later, his lip caught between his teeth in an expression that made Jaime want to lean over and kiss the abused flesh. The need to talk, to settle everything between them, held him back.

"You wanted to talk?" Jaime prompted.

Srikkanth nodded, taking the place next to Jaime on the couch. "I want another chance," he said. "I miss you. Sophie misses you."

"This can't be about Sophie," Jaime said with a shake of his head. "I love her and nothing will change that, but we can't be together because you need help with her. That isn't fair to her or to us."

"I know that," Srikkanth agreed. "I didn't mean it that way, but while it can't be about Sophie, anything we decide will affect her, and we can't forget that either."

"So what did you mean?"

Srikkanth took a deep breath. "I don't want to lose you. I want us to be together, like a proper couple."

"That isn't what you've been saying since the social worker visited," Jaime reminded him. "It isn't what you said on Friday night."

"I know," Srikkanth agreed, "and those fears aren't going to go away overnight, but I'll find a way to fight them. If you'll just give me another chance."

"I won't be a prisoner in my own house," Jaime warned him. "I can't live that way. If we're going to do this, I want us to be a normal couple, going out to eat or to the park or even just to the store together instead of skulking around like we're doing something wrong by being together."

Srikkanth swallowed hard, reminding himself that other gay couples managed all the time to lead normal lives, that he'd managed to lead a normal life before the fateful knock on the door, that he wanted Sophie to be as proud of him as he was of her. "Can we start with small things?" he asked. "I want us to have a normal life, but the fear doesn't just go away because I want it to."

"As long as you're trying," Jaime allowed. "I can only begin to imagine how hard it was for you, but you're letting the bigots win if you don't fight back by leading your life to the fullest. They can call all they want. Sophie isn't abused. She isn't neglected. She's as loved and as well-provided for as two people can possibly make her. She has her own room, plenty to eat, and two people who dote on her. Whoever called can call as often as they want. Nobody's going to take Sophie away from us just for being gay. We'd have to do something to hurt her before they could do that."

"I know," Srikkanth said. "The social worker even said she didn't care if we were gay as long as we were taking good care of Sophie. I'm not entirely ready to have the cops visiting regularly because some close-minded bastard keeps calling, but it's not fair to Sophie or to us for me to let that fear keep us inside."

"Us?" Jaime repeated, heart pounding with sudden hope.

"If you'll have me again," Srikkanth said timidly. "Fears and all."

"We all have fears," Jaime assured him. "It's how you deal with them that matters."

"I let the fact that Sophie was the one threatened keep me from dismissing this the way I've always dismissed people's prejudicial comments," Srikkanth explained. "If I don't protect her, who will?"

"We will," Jaime reminded him. "You said it the first night. We're stronger together than anything they can do to us. I just wish I knew who'd made the phone call in the first place. That little old lady across the parking lot always scowls at me when she sees me."

Srikkanth shook his head. "I don't think it was her. When I went to get groceries yesterday, she was outside walking her dog and asked me how my sweet girl was and why she hadn't seen her in awhile. I told her we must have missed her, and she said I should bring Sophie over to visit her some afternoon. I didn't know she could smile until the first time I saw her with Sophie."

"Maybe it was—"

"Don't," Srikkanth interrupted. "This line of conversation is as unproductive as my hiding. We don't know who it was, and we won't unless they approach us directly. Spending my time speculating on who might hate us enough to make such a call is just as bad as hiding here. It's still letting them win."

"You've done a lot of thinking since Friday night," Jaime observed.

"Yeah," Srikkanth said, "most of it in the last hour. I came home early, obviously, and panicked. I saw you in the park with the other guys."

"Paul and Jay," Jaime said. "They live a few blocks away with their son, Kyle. I've run into them in the park a couple of times, actually. They've been together for ten years and adopted Kyle six years ago when he was an infant. They told me about somewhere we could get help, actually, if we ever need it. There's an LGBT family center in town. I knew about the Gay Chamber of Commerce, but I guess I never bothered looking beyond that because I'm not particularly militant, but they said the center has helped several couples fight successful custody battles."

"That's reassuring," Srikkanth said. And it was, in a strange sort of way. He appreciated the reminder that he didn't have to face the bigots alone if it came to a fight for Sophie. He had an advantage adoptive gay couples didn't because of his biological tie to Sophie, but that was no guarantee. Knowing resources existed should he need them gave him the last push he needed to reach for Jaime's hand. "I've been miserable the past two days without you. Not because I needed you to help with Sophie, but because I missed you. Can we try again, without me being an idiot this time?"

"People are idiots all the time," Jaime said with a soft laugh, squeezing Srikkanth's hand. "It isn't whether we are but whether we work through it when we are."

"You're killing me here," Srikkanth protested. "Will you give me another chance?"

Jaime smiled and nodded, pulling Srikkanth closer so they could seal the bargain with a kiss. He'd intended it to be a quick kiss, but he hadn't counted on three days' worth of pent-up emotion and desire.

The moment their lips met, all other thought disappeared, everything except each other and the new and fragile bond the kiss affirmed. Srikkanth's breath was hot as it whispered across Jaime's lips, a shiver running through him. His tongue flicked out to wet his lips, only to be sucked into Srikkanth's mouth. He moaned softly, the sensation even more arousing than usual because of the swiftly fading tension from the three days of abstinence. He scooted closer to Srikkanth, releasing his grip on his boyfriend's hand in exchange for sliding his arms around the other man's waist. Srikkanth moved eagerly into the embrace, breaking away to murmur, "God, I've missed you."

"Me too," Jaime replied, no longer risking anything by admitting it. "I didn't sleep well the entire time I was down here alone. I've gotten used to having you next to me."

"I slept in Sophie's rocking chair," Srikkanth said with a pained laugh. "If you're up to it, I could use one of your wonderful massages."

Jaime grinned. "Then let's go upstairs. We'll be more comfortable in bed. If you don't mind?"

"Mind?" Srikkanth repeated. "I never wanted you anywhere else."

"I'll remember that," Jaime promised, rising to his feet and pulling Srikkanth with him. "Come on. Your bed is calling us."

Srikkanth led the way upstairs into his room, pulling Jaime back into his arms when they crossed the threshold. "We're going to make a new rule," he said as he leaned in to kiss Jaime again quickly. "No going to bed angry, even if we have to stay up all night to work something out, okay? I don't want to go through another weekend like this one ever again."

"It's a deal," Jaime agreed, not at all bothered by the idea that they might have other arguments. His parents argued sometimes, but they stood on a bedrock of belief in their marriage so solid that he never questioned whether they'd solve their problems. He wanted that same strength for Srikkanth and himself. "We'll turn my room into a play room for Sophie. That way we don't have anywhere to go but to bed together at night. How does that sound?"

"Pretty much perfect," Srikkanth said, his smile bright enough to light up the dreariest day. It certainly lightened Jaime's heart.

"Good, we'll work on the smaller stuff in the evenings and move furniture around on Sunday when we're both home," Jaime declared, "but for now, you wanted a massage." He nudged Srikkanth toward the bed. "Take off your shirt and lie down."

Srikkanth sent Jaime a flirtatious smile and pulled his tie off, tossing it in Jaime's direction as he started unbuttoning his shirt. Jaime watched in tense silence, waiting for the right moment to pounce. Inch after inch of mahogany skin came into view, tempting him to touch, but he held back until Srikkanth shrugged the shirt down his arms. Jaime surged forward, catching the shirt and using it to pin Srikkanth's arms in place as he kissed him hungrily, plundering the sweet cavern with every bit of built-up desire. He'd give Srikkanth the massage he'd promised, but only after he'd kissed him within an inch of his life.

Srikkanth's head fell back, cradled in one of Jaime's strong hands as he relaxed into the ravaging kiss. Jaime had never taken control like this, and it turned Srikkanth on beyond belief. Pliantly, he gave Jaime his mouth, basking in the other man's strength for this suspended moment in time. He could lean on Jaime, could rely on him to be there when Srikkanth needed him. At that moment, he was pretty sure he'd do whatever Jaime asked in return for another heady kiss. He wished he had his hands free to slide into Jaime's thick hair, but they were pinned behind his back by Jaime's grip on his shirt. He squirmed a little to get closer, and Jaime's grip tightened. Srikkanth wanted to tell Jaime that he wasn't trying to pull away, but he wasn't about to break the kiss to speak. He'd far rather let actions speak for him, rubbing against Jaime as best he could.

"God, I could just eat you up," Jaime muttered, breaking the kiss and propelling Srikkanth toward the bed.

"Fuck, yes," Srikkanth groaned. "Whatever you want. Anything you want."

Jaime's cock jumped in his jeans at the decadent offer, but he dismissed the images that sprang to mind. He didn't doubt Srikkanth's sincerity, but he didn't want the first time they made love to be make-up sex. He wanted it to be a slow, sweet seduction, so for tonight he'd settle for giving Srikkanth the promised massage and snuggling up beside him for the night. "What I want tonight is to work the knots out of your back and spoon up behind you and know I'm not alone."

Srikkanth sent him a disbelieving look, but Jaime indicated he should turn over with a twirl of his finger. Srikkanth pulled his shirt the rest of the way off and rolled onto his stomach as directed. Jaime crawled onto the bed, straddling Srikkanth's hips and deliberately ignoring the ache in his lower body. The heat of the dark skin surprised him as he spread his palms over the breadth of Srikkanth's shoulders, massaging gently at first, the force of his kneading increasing gradually as Srikkanth relaxed beneath his ministrations.

He worked his way down Srikkanth's back to the waistband of his slacks, hands bracketing his spine. He ignored the temptation to continue his downward progress, instead returning to Srikkanth's shoulders. He pressed a tender kiss to each shoulder blade before rolling to the side, pulling Srikkanth against him. "Feeling better?"

"I'd feel better if you fucked me," Srikkanth complained.

"We'll get there," Jaime assured him, "but only when we're both ready to take that step. Tonight, I'm not ready."

"But I thought you weren't mad at me anymore."

"I'm not," Jaime promised, "but we weren't having sex before our argument on Friday either, so it's not like I'm denying you something you'd gotten used to having. Making love is something special, Sri. Something sacred, even. And not treating it that way messes things up between people. We've messed up enough already. Let's make absolutely sure this is what we want so it doesn't mess us up."

CHAPTER FIFTEEN

SRIKKANTH couldn't quite stop the reflexive flinch when the doorbell rang despite his promise to Jaime to get over his fears. He'd dealt with most of it, going out to the park with Jaime and Sophie on several occasions, but something about the sound of the doorbell when he wasn't expecting anyone brought everything rushing back, even almost three months later. When he opened the door, a young Hispanic woman stood on the porch. "Hi, Srikkanth. You aren't dressed to go out yet. Didn't Jaime tell you I was coming?"

"Jaime isn't home from work yet," Srikkanth said, the pinch of fear replaced instantly by the bite of jealousy as he tried to figure out who the woman was and how she knew Jaime. His boyfriend had never given any indication of being bi, but that didn't necessarily guarantee anything. "What's going on?"

The girl rolled her eyes. "I'm Juana, Jaime's next youngest sister. He asked me if I'd babysit tonight so the two of you could go out somewhere nice without having to worry about your daughter. Show me around, why don't you, so I'll know where everything is if I need it."

Srikkanth smiled despite his confusion. Jaime had obviously arranged this as a surprise for him, to give them a "real" date, separate from their family outings. He hoped that meant maybe Jaime was ready to take the final step and do more than give him a quick hand job before snuggling up in bed with him at night. Whatever it meant, he certainly would take advantage of it. He hadn't been inside a four-star restaurant or a dance club since Sophie was born. He wouldn't trade her for anything, but with the opportunity in front of him again, he realized suddenly how much he'd missed some of the little luxuries he'd always taken for granted. Srikkanth stepped aside to let Juana inside. "Did he tell you where he was planning to go?"

"Well…" Juana hesitated.

"Don't tell me where if it's supposed to be a surprise," Srikkanth said. "Just tell me what I should wear."

Juana smiled. "Wear a tie. Show me where everything is and then go get ready. I'll take care of Sophie."

Srikkanth gave her a quick tour of the first floor, showing her where he kept the bottles and formula and going over the correct proportions for mixing them. He pointed out the playpen and bouncer as well as the blanket they spread on the floor when they played with Sophie there.

Taking her upstairs, he cracked the door to the nursery just as Sophie woke up. "I'll get her," Juana insisted. "Go take a shower, change clothes, do whatever it is gay men do before a hot date."

Srikkanth hesitated.

"She'll only cry harder if she sees you," Juana said. "Go. I've watched my nieces and nephews for years. I know what I'm doing."

Letting himself be convinced, Srikkanth retreated into his bedroom as Juana went into the nursery. He waited for the screech that usually accompanied a stranger approaching Sophie, but it didn't materialize. Relaxing, he went into the bathroom and took a quick shower, making sure everything was good and clean in case tonight was his lucky night.

Finished with his shower, he pulled on a pair of boxers and contemplated his closet blankly.

"Wear the black slacks and that maroon shirt your mother gave you for your birthday last year."

Srikkanth spun around to meet Jaime's eyes, the dark gaze sharp with desire.

"You didn't tell me you'd talked to your family about us," Srikkanth said hoarsely, not even trying to stop his reaction to Jaime's expression.

Jaime grimaced. "Not my family. Just Juana. She was the least freaked out when I told them I was gay. I figured she'd handle it best when I told her about Sophie. Besides, she loves to babysit."

"So where are we going?" Srikkanth asked as he took out the clothes Jaime had mentioned.

Jaime shook his head. "It's a surprise, but I promise you'll like it. And I promise Sophie will be in good hands."

"She didn't even cry when Juana got her up from her nap instead of me," Srikkanth admitted, starting to get dressed. "Do you need a shower?"

"No, I'll just change into something a little nicer than what I wear to work and we can go as soon as you're ready," Jaime replied.

Srikkanth buttoned his shirt. "I'm ready. Are you sure I shouldn't wear a different shirt so I can wear a tie?"

Jaime appraised Srikkanth's appearance with a lingering glance. "You could wear one if you want, but I rather like the open collar. It lets me imagine undoing your shirt one button at a time."

"Then I won't wear one," Srikkanth rasped. "Get changed. I'm ready."

Jaime didn't tease him about his sock feet. Srikkanth had never insisted his roommates or guests abide by the Indian custom of removing one's shoes at the door, but he never wore any shoes but slippers past the entryway of the condo.

Instead, Jaime grabbed a nicer pair of pants and shirt than he usually wore at work from his side of the closet and went into the bathroom to clean up a little before they went out. He'd hoped to get away early enough to shower, but they were cutting it close on their dinner reservations, and he didn't want to miss their table. He settled for washing his face and running a washcloth over his chest and groin to whisk away the worst of the sweat from the day before changing into the fresh clothes for dinner. He left the collar of his shirt open as well but grabbed a sports coat from the coat rack, deciding he wanted a bit more formality than the shirt alone.

"Are you sure I shouldn't change?" Srikkanth asked when he saw the jacket in Jaime's hand.

"I'm sure," Jaime said, giving him a quick kiss. "The needlework on that tunic makes it far dressier than what I'm wearing. And as I said, I want to imagine working it open. Come on. We're going to be late for dinner."

Srikkanth followed Jaime down the stairs, pausing at the foot of the steps to watch Sophie and Juana playing on the blanket on the floor. "There are emergency numbers on the refrigerator," he told Juana. "The pediatrician's office, the poison control center, my cell phone."

"Sri," Jaime chided.

"Thank you for telling me," Juana interrupted, shooting her brother a quelling glance. "It's always good to have all that information. I have Jaime's cell phone as well, obviously, if I need to get in touch with you. You two go and have a wonderful time and don't worry about a thing. Sophie and I will have fun together until you get back."

"She usually goes down around nine," Srikkanth warned.

"I'll make sure she's in bed on time," Juana promised. "Now go on. Enjoy your evening out."

Srikkanth slipped his shoes on and followed Jaime out to the car. "So where are we going?"

"You'll find out when we get there," Jaime said with a shake of his head. "Just relax and enjoy the evening."

There turned out to be the local Japanese steakhouse and hibachi grill. They arrived just in time to be seated. Jaime ordered drinks for both of them, waving aside Srikkanth's protest. "This is our first date without Sophie. Let me do things right."

"How about we do things right together?" Srikkanth proposed, consciously letting go of his worries at being away from Sophie. Jaime wouldn't have arranged the evening if Juana weren't perfectly capable of watching the baby for a few hours, which meant he really could relax and enjoy his time with his boyfriend.

Jaime smiled as the hostess explained the menu and the options for their dinner, slipping his hand beneath the table to find Srikkanth's. He wasn't sure how the other man would react, but Srikkanth simply turned his hand over and twined their fingers together.

They looked over the menu as the waitress brought their saké and took their salad orders. "What are you having?" Srikkanth asked after a moment.

"I can't decide between the teriyaki chicken and the shrimp," Jaime replied.

Srikkanth grinned. "Those were the two I was looking at too. You order one, I'll order the other, and we can share."

"I knew there was a reason I liked you," Jaime teased, returning the smile. "I hope you don't mind that I chose something like this rather than a table for two somewhere."

"I don't mind at all," Srikkanth said. "This is fun. We have plenty of privacy at home. It's nice to be out."

They sipped their drinks until the waitress returned with their salads and to take their orders. They laughed as they tried to eat their salads with chopsticks, but they refused to give in and pick up forks like some of the other people at their table. Then the hibachi chef arrived and they were too busy laughing and applauding to worry about eating anything.

When the show was finally over and their dinners set in front of them, Srikkanth looked at Jaime, his eyes luminous and his smile bright. "Thank you," he said, offering Jaime a bit of shrimp with his chopsticks. "I needed this."

Jaime smiled and leaned closer to take the morsel from Srikkanth's hand.

"Fuckin' queers."

Jaime and Srikkanth both looked up sharply, not sure which of the other men at the table had spoken. Srikkanth could feel his pulse pounding with dread at the thought of any kind of confrontation. He barely resisted drawing away from Jaime, but he reminded himself firmly that he had never been ashamed of being gay before Sophie was born, that his fears stemmed from the threat of losing her, not from any sense of wrongdoing.

"You know, some of us are trying to enjoy our meal," the woman next to Jaime said coldly to a man across the table, "including these gentlemen. So keep your opinions and your foul language to yourself."

The man looked like he was about to protest again, but his companion tugged on his arm, and he let himself be distracted. Srikkanth sighed in relief and turned his attention back to his meal.

"You all right?" Jaime murmured.

"Yeah," Srikkanth said, taking a bite of his shrimp. Mindful of the woman on Jaime's other side, he lowered his voice, leaning close so only Jaime could hear him. He pointedly ignored the glare that accompanied their renewed closeness. "I refuse to let ignorant pricks like that ruin my evening."

Jaime looked skeptical, but Srikkanth smiled and nodded.

"How's your chicken?" Srikkanth asked, deliberately changing the subject.

"Good," Jaime replied, a little surprised that Srikkanth was dealing with the comment this well, but he didn't press the issue, if only to keep from adding fuel to the fire. He didn't see any reason to ruin everyone else's meal because one person at their table was a homophobic jerk. "Have some."

Srikkanth glanced across the table at the man still glaring at them and decided he'd didn't want to change the way he and Jaime were acting. The man couldn't do anything except glare and make nasty comments in the restaurant, and those didn't have the power to do more than annoy him. Sophie wasn't with them, and they hadn't started pulling out baby pictures, so the man had no way of knowing about her. As long as he couldn't touch her, he couldn't touch Srikkanth in any appreciable way. With a grin for Jaime, he opened his mouth. "Let me have a taste."

The idiot, as Srikkanth had dubbed him mentally, kept the scowl in place for the rest of the meal, but he didn't say anything else and left as soon as he and his companion had finished eating. Srikkanth and Jaime lingered, enjoying their meal and dessert, sharing a clear chocolate martini and a huge pineapple boat.

When the woman next to Jaime, the one who'd defended them, rose to leave, she leaned over and said softly, "You two give me hope. My son is gay, but he's still young and wild. I'd like to see him in a real relationship some day, one like you have."

They thanked her, not sure what else to say. When she left, Jaime smiled at Srikkanth. "I think I like being part of something someone would want for their children."

They were alone at the table by that point, so Srikkanth didn't hesitate to give Jaime a light kiss. "Me too. Are you ready to go home?"

"Not yet," Jaime said with a shake of his head. "Our evening isn't over yet."

Srikkanth opened his mouth to ask about Sophie, but he pushed the concern aside. Jaime had surely told Juana how long he intended to be out. If she'd agreed to that, then the least he could do was enjoy Jaime's care in planning their date.

Jaime paid, adamantly refusing to let Srikkanth even see the total for the bill, insisting the evening was his treat. "Only if you let me pay next time," Srikkanth relented.

"Give me a day and time and I'll be there," Jaime promised.

Srikkanth refrained from naming the following Friday since he didn't have an easy babysitter the way Jaime did. He wondered if Juana would come if he called her instead of Jaime. He'd have to make sure to get her number before she left so he could return Jaime's surprise at some point.

"You're lost in thought," Jaime teased as the waitress returned with the receipt for Jaime to sign.

Srikkanth startled. "Sorry, just trying to work out the logistics of surprising you sometime."

"Babies do complicate things," Jaime agreed. "Let's go. I want to dance with you."

Jaime drove them to the trendiest dance club in town, one known for its tolerance of couples of any variation. Srikkanth had been there a few times, but not recently. He wasn't one to go out to a club to pick up a date, and it had been awhile since he'd had a steady boyfriend to go out with. He still couldn't quite believe he had one now.

The bouncer checked their IDs on the way in, not even blinking at Jaime's arm around Srikkanth's waist. Jaime ushered Sri inside, not bothering to look for a table. They weren't there to drink. He wanted to dance. Keeping his arm tight around Sri's waist, he led his boyfriend onto the dance floor. "Dance with me?"

Srikkanth smiled. "As long as you can put up with my two left feet."

Jaime started to sway to the music, a slow number at the moment. Srikkanth relaxed into his arms, letting him lead. Their bodies moved together easily, their familiarity with each other easing any awkwardness in the dance. Before long, Srikkanth buried his head in the curve of Jaime's neck, his lips trailing over smooth, honeyed skin, enjoying the scent of Jaime's cologne and the freedom to dance so closely.

The music changed, but Srikkanth didn't pull back for a more energetic dance, and Jaime didn't push him away, enjoying the closeness far too much to do anything that might disturb it. If Srikkanth decided he wanted to really dance at some point, Jaime wouldn't say no, but for now, he'd stay just as they were. He was far more interested in the press of Srikkanth's body against his than he was in the dancing.

The rest of the world ceased to exist for all the attention they paid to it, totally caught up in each other. Jaime's hands slid up and down Srikkanth's back, feeling the heat of his skin through the stiff silk of his tunic. Srikkanth reciprocated the caress, his hands slipping between the layers of Jaime's jacket and shirt. He was tempted to untuck the shirt in the back so he could find skin, but he didn't know if he'd be able to stop once he touched. The music pulsed around them, a rhythmic counterpoint to their quickening pulses as their bodies slid against one another, generating a heat from within that had nothing to do with the press of wildly gyrating bodies all around them. Their awareness of those other bodies, the outside noise, everything but the steady beat of the music and each other, faded to nothing as their kisses and caresses grew more intimate. The random contact between their bodies became more deliberate, Jaime's thigh pressing between Srikkanth's, applying friction firmly against his groin.

Srikkanth moaned softly and nuzzled Jaime's neck in the low light of the dance floor. Jaime turned his head obligingly and gave Srikkanth the kiss he had hoped for. Their lips clung the same way their bodies did, brushing, parting momentarily only to brush again seconds later, neither of them aware of the envious glances cast their way.

Eventually, sweet kisses gave way to lustier ones, tongues coming out to duel playfully as the moments of contact grew longer and the moments of separation came only when breathing was a necessity. "Let's go home," Jaime whispered, his breath sliding across Srikkanth's ear in another caress. He felt the shiver it evoked run the entire length of Srikkanth's body.

"We can continue this there, yeah?"

"All night long," Jaime promised.

CHAPTER SIXTEEN

JUANA met them at the door with a huge smile. "Sophie had a bottle about an hour ago and went right back to sleep."

"Great," Jaime said. "Thanks for watching her tonight."

"Any time."

"Say hi to Mamá for me on Sunday?" Jaime asked, switching to Spanish out of long habit with his family.

"You could come see her yourself," Juana scolded in kind. "She misses you."

Jaime shook his head. "You know she isn't comfortable with me. It's far easier for everyone if I stay away."

Juana bopped him on the head gently. "You haven't been to see her in so long that you don't know what she's comfortable with anymore. She was shocked—we all were—but she loves you the same as everyone else, and we've all made choices she would have preferred we not make."

"This wasn't a 'choice', Juana; it's who I am," Jaime reminded his sister.

"All the more reason to give her a chance to show you she's better now," Juana insisted.

Jaime frowned. Juana threw up her hands in defeat. "Fine, I'm going. Just promise me you'll think about it."

Jaime nodded to pacify her and shut the door behind her.

"Is everything all right?" Srikkanth asked, discarding his shoes at the door and coming up behind Jaime to put his arms around his boyfriend's waist. He'd picked up a little Spanish here and there over the years, but not enough to follow the rapid-fire conversation between brother and sister. "She didn't seem happy with you."

"She wants me to go see my mother," Jaime explained. "I haven't seen her except on Christmas and Easter since I told her I was gay. She didn't kick me out, but it obviously bothered her. It's easier for everyone if I'm not around all that much."

Srikkanth didn't know how to reply to that, his selective mention of his own sexuality with his family no help in giving Jaime advice. He changed the subject instead by nuzzling the nape of Jaime's neck. "Don't worry about it tonight. Let's go take advantage of Sophie being asleep."

Jaime nodded, leaning back into Srikkanth's arms, content for the moment to be the one comforted instead of the one doing the comforting. Relationships were like that, he reminded himself. You leaned on your partner when you were down and supported him when he was down. He'd spent most of the recent months supporting Srikkanth through the adjustment of having Sophie in his life. It wouldn't hurt him to lean a little now. Turning in Srikkanth's arms, he nuzzled the indention just below Sri's jaw. "I think that sounds like a marvelous idea. I want to make love with you."

That was the best idea Srikkanth had heard in months.

"What are we waiting for?" he joked, releasing his embrace so he could take Jaime's hand and lead him toward the stairs. They'd have to be quiet upstairs so they wouldn't disturb Sophie, but he didn't mind. He wanted the first time they made love to be in their bed, not in the spare bedroom/playroom.

"You tell me," Jaime teased, following willingly, his mind already racing with everything he wanted to do to Srikkanth. Starting with peeling him out of that tunic.

"Nothing at all," Srikkanth replied, leading Jaime into the bedroom and turning to renew their embrace. "Not one damn thing."

He pushed at the collar of Jaime's jacket, wanting it off so he could get to the shirt and then to the skin beneath.

Jaime shrugged out of the linen garment, letting it fall unheeded to the floor. He'd pick it up later. Right now, he had only one focus. Getting them both naked as quickly as possible.

He worked at the fastenings down the front of Srikkanth's tunic, frowning a little as he struggled to release the knotted cords that replaced buttons on the front. The couple of drinks he'd had with dinner and while they were dancing didn't help, his fingers fumbling awkwardly.

"Here, let me," Srikkanth said with a grin, releasing the clasp at the back of the collar and pulling the tunic over his head. "They're not just for decoration, but you don't actually have to open them to take it off."

"Now you tell me," Jaime muttered, but his voice held no real heat. How could it when Srikkanth's smooth, dark chest beckoned so enticingly? Pulling the other man back into his arms, he slid his lips along the curve of Srikkanth's shoulder and then down toward one mahogany nipple. "You smell good," he murmured against Sri's skin.

"Your sister insisted I take a shower before we went out," Srikkanth gasped.

Jaime smiled. "She's occasionally good for something."

Yeah, like babysitting, Srikkanth thought, but the words didn't make it to his lips. Jaime's mouth on his nipple stole his concentration and his will to do anything but tremble with desire in his lover's arms. He moaned softly, biting his lip to keep the sound from growing louder as Jaime's tongue swiped across his pebbling flesh. His cock, which had softened during the drive home and Jaime's conversation with Juana, hardened again swiftly, the stimulation exactly what he craved. His fingers carded through Jaime's hair, encouraging him to linger, to use more pressure, to move to the other side. It didn't matter as long as he didn't stop.

Fortunately, Jaime didn't seem to have any intention of stopping, his hands firm on Srikkanth's hips to hold him in place as he lavished attention on both sensitive buds. Making sure to draw his lover with him so Jaime wouldn't think he was pulling away, Srikkanth backed toward the bed, wanting to get them both horizontal as quickly as possible. They'd have more freedom that way. Besides, he wanted to feel Jaime's weight pressing him into the mattress again.

Jaime didn't mind the suggestion at all, pulling away for a moment when Srikkanth reached the bed to remove his boyfriend's slacks, leaving him clad only in his boxers, the front tented by the growing bulge of Srikkanth's erection.

"You can take those off too," Srikkanth offered with a nod of his head toward his shorts.

"I will," Jaime promised, "but not just yet. I don't want this to be over too quickly, and that's what would happen with you completely naked in bed."

"We have all night."

"So we do," Jaime conceded, reaching for the waistband of Srikkanth's boxers. "But don't say I didn't warn you."

Srikkanth lifted his hips to facilitate his disrobing, the movement too much of an enticement for Jaime to resist. He lowered his head, capturing the tip of Srikkanth's cock in his mouth, sucking lightly as he finished stripping the recumbent man.

"Oh, fuck," Srikkanth groaned.

Jaime chuckled and lifted his head momentarily. "We will, but I'm going to enjoy you first."

"Not fair," Srikkanth protested. "I can't reach you. Get undressed and then come up here so I can return the favor."

Jaime thought that sounded like a marvelous idea, so he rose long enough to finish pulling off his clothes. He returned to the bed, his feet near Srikkanth's head. Srikkanth grabbed his hips, urging him up onto his knees so that his cock dangled in Srikkanth's face. "Perfect. And all mine."

"All yours," Jaime agreed, gasping a little when Srikkanth started licking at him. "And this is all mine." His hands closed possessively over Srikkanth's ass as he lowered his head to nuzzle his groin. Srikkanth didn't reply, but his moan vibrated around Jaime's cock, sending a shiver up Jaime's back and blood rushing downward. Determined to give Srikkanth as much pleasure as he was receiving, he went to work on the thick shaft, licking it from base to tip and back again. Srikkanth shivered beneath him even as he sucked Jaime's cock into his mouth, his hands settling on Jaime's hips to hold him in place.

Jaime reciprocated, bobbing his head up and down on Srikkanth's erection, letting the tip nudge the back of his throat each time without actually taking it all the way down. It was enough to drive Srikkanth wild, the caress that was never quite enough, never quite all. He bucked beneath Jaime's mouth, trying to get deeper, to bury himself down Jaime's throat. Jaime's hands stopped him, though, keeping the suction shallow, focusing on the head of his cock.

Srikkanth shuddered, trying to hold back, but the constant stimulation was too much. With a shout muffled by Jaime's cock in his mouth, he climaxed hard.

The jet of hot cream against Jaime's throat surprised him, some of it dribbling out as he swallowed reflexively. Not wanting to miss even a drop of the salty treat, he released the still-twitching cock and worked his way lower, over Srikkanth's relaxing balls to lap around his entrance. He could smell the sweat from their dancing, taste the salt. It only added to the intimacy.

Then Srikkanth's fingers slid into Jaime's crease, circling his entrance, and Jaime's orgasm blindsided him. His knees gave out, and he collapsed onto Srikkanth's body, nuzzling the inside of his lover's thigh tenderly. Srikkanth stroked the back of his knee in return, sending a renewed curl of desire up Jaime's spine.

He pushed back up onto his knees, ignoring Srikkanth's sound of protest, intending to turn around so he could kiss the other man and see about reviving his interest as well. Sophie's wail in the next room derailed that plan. Srikkanth had squirmed out from beneath Jaime before he could even suggest that he'd take care of her. Deciding he didn't want to be away from Srikkanth for the time it would take him to feed Sophie, he pulled on his sleep pants and followed his lover into the nursery.

"She's burning up," Srikkanth said as he bent to pick Sophie up from her crib.

"Get her bottle ready and I'll get the thermometer," Jaime replied, hurrying into the bathroom and digging through the drawer for the thermometer. Bringing it back, he slipped it under her arm while Jaime rocked her and tried to convince her to take the bottle. She settled to it after a few minutes, but her sucking was fitful, and she was obviously uncomfortable. When the thermometer beeped, it read 100.3. "She has a bit of a fever," Jaime told Srikkanth. "I'll get the Tylenol."

"Should we call the doctor?" Srikkanth asked worriedly. He wanted to believe everything was fine. Juana hadn't said anything about Sophie being fussy or feverish before she left, and even though he'd just met her, she hadn't struck him as someone who would forget to mention that sort of detail. She would have mentioned it if Sophie had been sick earlier.

"Not yet," Jaime reassured him. "It's not a very high fever, and it just started. We'll keep an eye on her and see how she does tonight. If it spikes or if she gets worse, we'll call. Otherwise we'll see how she is in the morning. Just keep rocking her while I get her medicine."

Srikkanth nodded and turned his attention back to Sophie. He had a passing thought for their interrupted plans for the night, but there would be other nights. Sophie needed him—them—now, and that was far more important.

Jaime hurried downstairs to the cabinet where they kept all the medicines and got the infant Tylenol and Motrin. He'd take them both back upstairs in case Sophie needed another dose during the night. She was still taking her bottle when he returned to the nursery, so he sat down on the daybed and waited for her to finish. When she was done, he gave her the thick syrup. "Babies get fevers sometimes," Jaime reminded Srikkanth, seeing the panicked look on his boyfriend's face. "It might be an ear infection or a mild virus, or it might just be a tummy ache. Most of the time, they're really minor and better within twenty-four hours. Do you want to see if she'll go back to bed?"

Srikkanth shook his head, not at all to Jaime's surprise, though the expression on his face did relax somewhat at Jaime's encouragement.

"Then let's take her with us back in the other room. You'd be uncomfortable sitting up in here all night, and there isn't really room in the daybed for all three of us."

"You don't have to stay," Srikkanth said.

"I know I don't," Jaime replied, stroking Srikkanth's shoulder encouragingly, "but we're in this together now. If we're going to be together, then she's going to be my daughter too. Come on. We'll be more comfortable in bed. We can put her between us so she won't roll out and then snuggle together, all three of us."

Srikkanth rose and followed Jaime back into the bedroom. At Jaime's direction, he stripped Sophie down to her diaper. "So she won't get overheated between us," Jaime explained when Srikkanth shot him a questioning look. "She's already feverish. We don't want to make it worse."

"Maybe she shouldn't sleep in here," Srikkanth hesitated. "Maybe I should sleep in the other room with her."

"You can," Jaime said slowly, reminding himself that Srikkanth was still relatively new to being a father and that his concern for Sophie was a tribute to his sense of responsibility rather than a rejection, "but I'd really like to hold you tonight. I suppose we could try to squeeze into the daybed."

Srikkanth considered the logistics for a moment, but there was no way two grown men could sleep comfortably in the daybed. "No, we'll stay here," he decided. "I'm worrying for nothing probably. We'll be more comfortable here and we can keep an eye on Sophie at the same time. It won't hurt her to sleep with us for one night."

"It wouldn't hurt even if it was more than one night," Jaime assured him. "Although I have to admit, I won't complain about being able to hold you close to me again when she's better. We have some unfinished business still."

"Sophie—"

"Sophie is sick and that's more important," Jaime interrupted. "As it should be. But when she's better and back in her own bed, I intend to make good on that promise of loving you all night long."

Srikkanth smiled as he settled Sophie on the bed between them, making sure she wouldn't fall between the pillows and have trouble breathing during the night. "I'm looking forward to it."

Jaime climbed in bed on the other side, kissed Sophie's forehead gently and then leaned across her so he could kiss Srikkanth. Their lips clung with the promise of nights to come.

Chapter Seventeen

"Hello?"

"What do you mean telling your sister you have a baby and not telling me?"

Jaime held the phone out away from his ear as his mother's spate of scolding came pouring across the line. "Mamá," he said, trying to get a word in edgewise.

The stream of Spanish continued, his mother berating him for not calling her, not coming to see her, not telling her what was going on in his life. "And a granddaughter! Why didn't you tell me I had a granddaughter?"

"Mamá!" Jaime said more forcefully. "Mamá, *por favor*, listen to me!"

His mother finally ran out of steam, letting him have his say. "Mamá, it's complicated," he began.

"No, it's not," she insisted. "You have a baby. Your sister saw her. You didn't tell me about her. It's not complicated."

"It is complicated," Jaime repeated. "Sophie isn't my daughter, legally or biologically. She's Srikkanth's daughter. You remember my housemate, the one I'm renting a room from?"

"*Sí*, but Juana said she watched her for you. Why would she watch your housemate's baby?"

Jaime took a deep breath, steeling himself for his mother's disapproval. "Because I wanted to take Srikkanth out to dinner without Sophie."

"That's nice of you, *mi hijo*. You always were a considerate boy. Why did Juana tell me she was your baby?"

"Because I wasn't being considerate, Mamá. I was taking my boyfriend out on a date," Jaime said with a sigh, sure that would be the end of their conversation.

"So is this serious or is he someone you just mess around with?" his mother asked after a long pause.

"It's serious, Mamá," Jaime assured her.

"Good. You don't mess around with someone who has a baby. That person needs someone to help, not to distract."

Eyebrows lifting in surprise, Jaime nodded before realizing his mother couldn't see him. "I know that, Mamá. Your lectures rubbed off on me, even if I never expected to be in a situation where I'd be with someone who had a child. I'm helping him take care of Sophie, but I'm only around so much, and I wanted him to have a night off. That's why I called Juana."

His mother harrumphed again. "You call your sister, but you didn't call me. Bring them to dinner on Sunday. I want to meet this special someone. And the baby."

"Mamá."

She hung up before he could finish his sentence.

With a sigh, Jaime put the phone back on the cradle and went in search of Srikkanth. It sounded like he had some explaining to do. And an invitation to extend.

He found Srikkanth and Sophie sitting on the floor of her playroom building with blocks. Srikkanth would make a tower and Sophie would knock them over and giggle gleefully. Jaime smiled. It was hard to believe she was already seven months old and sitting on her own.

"Did the phone ring?" Srikkanth asked when he looked up and saw Jaime in the doorway.

"Yes, it was my mother," Jaime began. "My sister apparently has a big mouth."

Srikkanth's face tightened at the odd tone in Jaime's voice. "Are you all right?"

Jaime shrugged. "I think so. The question is whether you'll be all right."

"Why wouldn't I be?" Srikkanth asked.

"My mother has 'invited' us to dinner on Sunday," Jaime explained. "All three of us."

"But that's wonderful," Srikkanth said, rising to his feet. "It means she's not as bothered by your orientation as you feared."

"Maybe," Jaime allowed, "but it's a command performance, and those never make me happy."

Srikkanth shook his head and crossed to Jaime's side, his arms going around his lover's waist. "It's an olive branch. Take it. We'll all get dressed up and go over and meet your mother. If it goes well, you'll get to see your family more often, and if it doesn't, it's one afternoon in the rest of our lives. We can make that sacrifice on the chance that it will work out. It would be nice to have their support as Sophie gets older. She won't have grandparents around on my side of the family. Jill didn't have any family left. Your family is all Sophie has."

"That's a low blow," Jaime said, but he smiled as he spoke, taking the heat out of the words. "We'll give them a chance. Maybe it won't be that bad."

Jaime let himself be persuaded, joining Sophie on the floor to see how high he and Srikkanth could build the tower before she knocked it over.

"TELL me everyone's name again," Srikkanth requested as they drove to Jaime's mother's house for lunch.

"I don't know for sure who will be there," Jaime replied, "but my mother, obviously, and you've already met Juana. My oldest brother, Alvaro, will be there too. He and his wife Paula live with Mamá since my father died. They never had any kids. I don't know if my oldest sister, Beatriz, will be there. She lives farther away than the rest of us. She isn't married yet, much to Mamá's dismay. There's also Lourdes and her husband, Vicente, and their two boys, Martin and Damian. And then there are the babies, well, my baby brother and sister, Luis and Diana. They're still teenagers. Alvaro would never admit it, of course, being the good Latino that he is, but I think he's ready for them to go off to college so they're not under foot all the time."

Srikkanth laughed. "I probably won't remember a word of that when we get there, but I'll get it eventually."

"If they let us come back."

"Jaime," Srikkanth scolded, "stop being negative. If you go in there with that kind of attitude, it's going to rub off on them and this won't work. Your mother invited you. The afternoon will probably be tense, but she wouldn't have called if she didn't want to see you."

"She wants to see Sophie," Jaime corrected.

Srikkanth shrugged. "Good. She'll see you at the same time, and since she only gets Sophie if she takes you and me in the bargain, maybe that'll be enough for things to start getting better."

"I don't want you to think I'm using you and Sophie—"

"Stop right there," Srikkanth interrupted. "You're not using anyone. If anything, I'm using you for the knowledge and support you can give me. And don't tell me I'm not. I know I'm not. We're past that stage now. We're a couple, a unit. A family. If that helps make things better between you and your family, how could I not be happy about that? Anything that makes you happier makes us stronger."

"I'm glad you feel that way," Jaime said. "Truly. I miss my family, but it was easier to just leave things alone. Maybe things won't get any better, but at least this has broken the stalemate."

"Then let's go see what we can do to make things better," Srikkanth said as they arrived at Jaime's family's house. He leaned over and kissed Jaime lightly. "I won't be able to do that inside, but I'll be thinking about it the whole time, wishing I could show my support physically as well as emotionally."

Jaime smiled, the first one that felt real to him since his mother had called. "I'm really lucky, you know that. A gorgeous, supportive boyfriend and a precious baby girl. I don't think life could get much better."

The door to the house opened, and Juana came out onto the porch. "You two gonna sit there all day or come inside and see everyone? Mamá's been cooking since lunch yesterday. She even made tamales for you, Jaime."

Jaime's eyes widened. "Those are my favorite," he told Srikkanth. "Maybe this won't be as bad as I feared."

Srikkanth unbuckled his seatbelt and got out, taking Sophie's carseat from the back so they could use it as a crib when she was ready for her nap. She gurgled up at him. "Hi, beautiful," he said to Juana when she came out to the car.

Juana grinned at him. "Buttering me up?"

"I'm not about to alienate the one person who's on my side," Srikkanth confided. "Jaime's worried this is going to be a miserable afternoon."

Juana shook her head. "I don't think so. Alvaro hasn't come around yet, but his wife is excited about the baby and so's Mamá. Give them time."

"What about everyone else?"

"It varies, but Mamá and Alvaro are the two you need to worry about," Juana explained. "If they approve of you, everyone else will follow suit sooner or later."

Srikkanth nodded as Jaime joined them. "Telling secrets about me?" he asked as he bent to kiss Juana's cheek.

"Not at all," Juana replied smoothly. "I'm just hitting on your boyfriend."

Jaime spluttered as Juana took Srikkanth's arm and led him toward the house. He trailed along behind, wondering when his sister had gotten so bossy.

"Mamá," Juana called as she stepped inside, "Jaime's here."

Within seconds, it seemed, the living room went from being deserted to overflowing with people, all milling around as they tried to decide where to sit or stand. Srikkanth set Sophie's carseat down and busied himself with taking her out while he waited to see how everyone would react to Jaime.

"Jaime," the clear patriarch said with a stiff nod. "It's been a long time."

Jaime nodded back, offering his hand, which his brother took slowly. "Too long," Jaime agreed.

"Mamá misses you. Don't let it happen again." Before Jaime could reply to that, his brother had turned and walked away without acknowledging Srikkanth.

Jaime started to protest, but it was forestalled by his mother's embrace. Jaime didn't say anything, simply holding her and being held. She smelled exactly the way he remembered: of flour and jasmine. Sophie's giggle at being lifted from her seat broke the spell, and *Señora* Frias came bustling over to Srikkanth.

"Let me see the little *niña*," she cooed, reaching for Sophie. Srikkanth handed her over without protest, suspecting Sophie would do his job for him if he let her. *Señora* Frias held her with the experience of a woman with seven children, and Sophie smiled up at her, clearly content.

"I think she likes you," Srikkanth commented with a quiet smile.

"All babies like my mamá," Jaime explained, coming to stand next to Srikkanth as his mother rocked Sophie, crooning to her in rapid-fire Spanish.

"Of course they do," *Señora* Frias said. "They know I like them. Come with me, *angelita*. I teach you how to make tortillas."

She disappeared through the door to the kitchen before either man could say another word. Srikkanth glanced at Jaime, who smiled reassuringly. "Let me introduce you to everyone," he said.

Srikkanth took a deep breath and summoned his best smile as Jaime led him deeper into the living room. "Srikkanth, this is my sister-in-law, Paula."

"Nice to meet you, Paula," Srikkanth said, extending his hand.

"Nice to meet you as well, Srikkanth. Juana hasn't stopped talking about Sophie in days," Paula said, shaking his hand. "She says Sophie is a much easier baby than my nephews were."

"She has her moments," Srikkanth allowed, "but yes, most of the time, she's a little darling."

"So you're Jaime's landlord?" one of the others asked.

"No, Vicente," Jaime broke in before Srikkanth could decide how to reply, "Srikkanth is my boyfriend."

"Oh, but I thought…." He trailed off awkwardly.

"Don't think," the woman standing next to him said. "I'm Lourdes, Jaime's sister. I'm glad you're here, even if my husband doesn't know when to keep his mouth shut."

"It's fine," Srikkanth assured her. "Jaime did rent a room from me for three years, so it's not like he was entirely wrong."

Lourdes shot another glare at her husband. "He knows that. He's being obtuse. How old is your daughter?"

"Seven months," Srikkanth replied, eager for a safer topic.

"That's when they start being fun," Lourdes said. "My boys are four and six. They're running around here somewhere, probably downstairs because that's where their *abuela* keeps the video games she tells me she doesn't let them play. Hopefully Luis is making sure they're only playing the ones for younger kids."

"Luis is my youngest brother," Jaime reminded Srikkanth. "He's sixteen. The boys adore him."

"Because he lets them get away with anything they want," Vicente said sourly.

Everyone ignored him.

"Juana!" *Señora* Frias's voice broke into the silence.

Juana disappeared into the kitchen and returned a moment later with Sophie in her arms. "Mamá says dinner will be ready in fifteen minutes." Before Srikkanth could ask if she wanted him to take Sophie, she'd deposited the baby on Alvaro's lap. "She said for you to hold the baby until dinner."

That forestalled any protest on anyone's part, but it didn't stop Srikkanth from holding his breath to see how Alvaro would react. Alvaro, however, didn't even blink, simply setting Sophie on his lap and bouncing her gently, his countenance transformed from its previous stern expression to one of sweet delight as Sophie laughed and clapped her hands.

"See?" Srikkanth murmured as the tension in the room suddenly dropped by several degrees. "I told you Sophie would do our work for us."

Jaime chuckled. "You're brilliant."

Conversation returned slowly to normal levels, the family catching up with each other's news from the week. The sounds swirled around Srikkanth, most of the conversation taking place in Spanish. He had a feeling he'd be learning the language in self-defense. He drew back a little, watching Jaime being drawn slowly back into the circle of family. It was awkward at first, but these were Jaime's brothers and sisters, and the family was obviously close-knit. As they continued to talk, he could see the awkwardness fade. Srikkanth tensed again when Alvaro rose, Sophie on his hip, but

Alvaro simply juggled her and patted Jaime on the shoulder as he walked by.

"Your daughter is beautiful," Alvaro said, coming to stand beside Srikkanth. "You are very lucky to have her."

"I know I am," Srikkanth agreed, remembering how close he'd come to giving her up for adoption. "I'm sorry her mother died, but I'm not sorry I have her."

"Jaime didn't explain that. You are... like him, *sí*? And yet you have a daughter."

Srikkanth laughed softly. "Yes, I'm gay like Jaime. Sophie's mother, Jill, was my best friend. When she wanted to have a baby, I went to the fertility clinic with her. She died giving birth to Sophie, and suddenly I had a daughter."

Alvaro nodded. "You're a very busy man, then. What do you do with her while you're at work?"

"I work from home most days," Srikkanth explained, "so I can watch Sophie at the same time. Jaime juggled his schedule so he's home on Mondays when I have to go into the office. It's not ideal since it means he has to work on Saturdays, but it's better than having her in a daycare where I wouldn't get to see her all day."

"That won't work much longer," Alvaro warned. "I don't have children, but I have younger brothers and sisters. In another month, Sophie won't stay where you put her. When you need someone to watch her during the day, you call Mamá or Paula. They don't work. They'll be glad to have a baby in the house."

"I couldn't impose like that," Srikkanth protested.

Alvaro gave a very Latin shrug. "It isn't an imposition when it's family."

"Dinner!" *Señora* Frias called from the kitchen.

"I'll take her," Srikkanth offered.

Alvaro laughed. "We're experts at eating and holding babies. We'll just pass her around the table."

They made their way into the dining room to the huge table groaning beneath all the dishes. Srikkanth counted at least twelve different platters on the table: tamales, beans, tortillas, some kind of chicken, and several dishes he couldn't identify. It all smelled delicious.

"You won't want the enchiladas," Jaime murmured at Srikkanth's side, "but I think that's the only beef dish."

"Thanks," Srikkanth replied softly. He wasn't terribly strict in his dietary practices, much to his parents' dismay, but he'd never developed a taste for beef.

The family started passing the dishes around, the conversation continuing unabated, only in English now. Srikkanth wondered if that meant he'd been accepted.

"So where do you work?" Luis asked Srikkanth.

"I'm a web designer," Srikkanth explained. "The company contracts with all sorts of local businesses to design and maintain their web sites. At the moment, I'm working on a redesign for The Corkscrew."

"I love that store," Paula exclaimed. "I shop there at least once a month."

"After this month, you'll be able to order online and have the order boxed and ready when you come to pick it up," Srikkanth confided. "That's one of the things I'm building into the new site."

"Wines only? Or will it have their other products as well?" Paula asked.

"They'll make that decision when they input the actual inventory themselves, but the site is set up to accommodate multiple categories of products and to allow for searches so you can find a specific product by name," Srikkanth revealed.

"That's so cool," Diana enthused. "I'm taking a web design course as an elective this year, but school just started, so we're still learning the basics."

"If you need any help, let me know," Srikkanth offered.

"Would you be willing to be a guest speaker?" Diana asked excitedly. "Mr. Robinson said just the other day that he'd like to have someone come talk to us about careers in web design."

"Sure," Srikkanth agreed. "Here; give him my card and have him call me. As long as it's not a Monday, I can arrange the time, although I'd have to find a babysitter."

"You don't need babysitter," *Señora* Frias interjected. "You tell me what day and you bring the *niña* here. Or if you prefer, I come to your house."

"You don't have to do that, Mrs. Frias," Srikkanth protested.

"You go to help my daughter in class; I keep *mi nieta* for you," *Señora* Frias declared. "You tell me when."

"*Gracias*, Mamá," Jaime said before Srikkanth could reply, his voice hoarse with emotion at hearing his mother claim Sophie as her granddaughter.

"*De nada, niño. Come.*"

Jaime did as he was told, digging into his overflowing plate. Juana was right, he realized. He'd done them all a disservice by staying away so long. "So can we come back next week, Mamá?"

"Silly boy," *Señora* Frias scolded. "You come back every week if your friend stops calling me *señora* and calls me Mamá like everyone else."

CHAPTER EIGHTEEN

"AND you were worried," Srikkanth teased as they drove home at the end of the evening.

"It went far better than I expected," Jaime agreed. "We don't have to go every Sunday if you don't want to."

"Why wouldn't I want to?" Srikkanth asked. "Your family was lovely, and Sophie was a big hit."

"God, I love you," Jaime blurted out, eyes widening as he realized what he'd let slip.

Srikkanth flinched. "Don't say that if you don't mean it."

"I mean it," Jaime insisted. "I don't know why I didn't say it a long time ago. It just didn't seem to be the right time."

"Pull over," Srikkanth demanded. "Into a driveway, into a parking lot, I don't care."

"What?" Jaime asked, surprised.

"Pull over," Srikkanth repeated. "I need to kiss you. Right now."

Jaime's eyes widened even more as he searched for a spot to pull over. Finding a parking lot, he drove in and put the car in park, releasing his seatbelt as he did. He reached for Srikkanth even as Srikkanth pulled him into a tight embrace, their mouths crashing together. Jaime gasped into the torrid kiss, head spinning as Srikkanth kissed him with more fervor, more passion than ever before.

"Say it again," Srikkanth demanded, breaking the kiss momentarily.

"I love you," Jaime repeated.

Srikkanth took a deep breath, eyes closing. "I love you too."

Jaime relaxed muscles he didn't even know he'd tensed at the words he'd longed to hear. "Can we go home now? I want to put Sophie to bed and then take you there. And tonight, nothing's going to stop me from making love to you."

"Not even Sophie?" Srikkanth teased.

"Not even Sophie," Jaime replied firmly. "Not tonight, when I finally know you love me too."

"Then let's go home," Srikkanth agreed.

Jaime drove home as quickly as safety would allow, the thought of the baby asleep in the back seat enough to temper his urge to hurry. They carried her car seat inside, leaving her strapped in securely so she wouldn't roll out while she slept, rather than waking her to move her into her crib. When she wanted a bottle, they could transfer her to her bed.

As soon as she was settled, Jaime reached for Srikkanth, pulling him into a tender embrace. His heart pounding in his chest, he nuzzled his boyfriend's jaw, lips sliding back to the tender skin beneath his ear. Srikkanth shivered in his arms, bringing a smile to Jaime's lips even as he intensified his attentions. He wanted Srikkanth incapable of doing anything other than moaning and coming apart in his arms. Over and over and over again, if he had his way.

Waltzing Srikkanth backward into their bedroom, Jaime released the other man for a moment to switch on a dim lamp and light one of the incense sticks that rested on the dresser. He hadn't told Srikkanth he loved him in the way he would've preferred, so he'd have to make the first time they made love perfect instead. He could feel Srikkanth's eyes on his back, could almost hear his lover urging him to stop messing around and hurry up, but Jaime resisted the silent entreaty. This wasn't some casual fling, a meaningless release. This was Srikkanth, and Jaime intended to treat this moment with the reverence it deserved.

The setting arranged to his satisfaction, Jaime returned to Srikkanth's side, wrapping his arms around Srikkanth's waist, swaying side to side until his boyfriend's feet moved in time with his own. He guided them slowly toward the bed, his hands wandering over Srikkanth's back as they moved. The smell of incense wrapped around their senses, adding to the weight of the moment. When Srikkanth's thighs bumped against the edge of the bed, Jaime stilled his feet, his hands burrowing beneath his lover's shirt to find smooth skin.

Growing impatient with the slow pace, Srikkanth reared back enough to pull his polo over his head, baring his chest in the hopes of enticing Jaime into more intimate contact. To his frustration, Jaime simply smiled and returned to kissing him and stroking his back. Not that it didn't feel good, of course, but Srikkanth wanted more. Now.

He worked his hands beneath Jaime's button-down shirt, determined to speed things along. Finding the bottom button, he freed it from its hole and moved upward, opening Jaime's shirt in reverse so their chests met with soft friction as he pushed the garment down Jaime's arms and onto the floor.

The contact shouldn't have been unusually electrifying— they'd slept side by side for weeks in nothing but their boxers and had been completely naked together on more than one occasion— yet this felt different, more powerful, as if the confession of their shared emotion had heightened the sensation. Jaime shifted slowly, brushing his smooth skin against Srikkanth's chest, enjoying the rasp of his lover's light pelt on his sensitive nipples. He lowered his head to the curve of Srikkanth's dark shoulder, trailing his lips along the curve of his collarbone and then on to brush across one taut peak. He licked teasingly at the mahogany nipple, smiling as Srikkanth moaned. The smell of Srikkanth's cologne was strong there, the musky scent mingling with the smoke from the incense to intoxicate Jaime's senses. His hands keeping Srikkanth close, he lowered his lover to the bed, never breaking the contact between his lips and the other man's skin. Urging Srikkanth to move up so he lay fully on the bed, Jaime crawled over him on hands and knees so he could continue to titillate Srikkanth's skin.

"You don't have to seduce me," Srikkanth rasped. "I'm a sure thing."

Jaime chuckled. "I'm glad to hear that, but that's all the more reason to seduce you, you know. We've done everything backward, but we're here now, and I intend to take my time."

"Backward?" Srikkanth asked, trying to hold on to his train of thought as Jaime tugged on his socks and began unzipping his pants.

"We had the baby first," Jaime explained, stripping Srikkanth down to his boxers. "The family is usually what comes last, not first. I'm not complaining. I wouldn't change a thing even if I could, but making love to you is long overdue, and I'm going to make up for lost time by doing it right."

Srikkanth didn't think there was any way it could be wrong between them, but he didn't have the breath to voice that opinion with Jaime nuzzling his cock through his shorts. His eyes closed on a soft moan as he lifted his hips, inviting more attention.

Jaime traced the bulge of Srikkanth's cock through the thin fabric. "As good as I know you'd taste, I'm not falling into that trap again," he warned Srikkanth. "I'd start sucking on you and forget about everything else, and tonight I want to know what it feels like to be inside you."

"Yes," Srikkanth groaned. "Want that too."

Jaime breathed a sigh of relief. He hadn't been absolutely sure he'd read Srikkanth correctly. While he wasn't opposed to bottoming—he rather enjoyed it, in fact—he needed to be the one in charge tonight. He couldn't have explained why if Srikkanth had asked, but it seemed his lover shared the same need.

"Lube… in the drawer," Srikkanth said with a toss of his head as Jaime reared back onto his knees to finish undressing himself.

Tossing his clothes aside, Jaime tugged the drawer open, digging through it in search of the promised lube and, hopefully, a stray condom or two. He had some in the downstairs bathroom, but he really didn't want to pull away long enough to go get them. Silently kicking himself for not taking a detour on the way upstairs in the first place, he frowned when he couldn't find the lube. "Are you sure?"

Pushing up on one elbow, Srikkanth pulled the drawer farther out, finally finding the lube all the way in the back, along with a lone condom packet. "It's been awhile since I've needed them," Srikkanth explained with a diffident shrug. "I guess I'll have to restock."

"We'll bring some up from downstairs," Jaime said. "Tomorrow."

Srikkanth nodded his agreement, not in any hurry to move from his comfortable spot on the bed, Jaime hovering over him, about to make love to him finally. If they needed another condom before morning, they could go get one then. For now, he preferred to concentrate on this moment, this experience. Lifting his head, he nipped at the line of muscle bisecting Jaime's honeyed abdomen, loving the contrast between his dark hands and Jaime's lighter skin. The thought brought a smile to his face, for Jaime was hardly light-skinned, except when compared to Srikkanth. "Love you," Srikkanth murmured against Jaime's belly.

"Love you too," Jaime replied, setting the lube and condom next to them on the bed where they wouldn't get lost. He took a moment to simply drown in Srikkanth's near-black eyes, wondering how he'd gotten so lucky as to have this beautiful man as a lover. Bending his head, he brushed his lips over Srikkanth's again and again, enjoying the lingering taste of spices. "Love you, love you, love you," he whispered between passes. "So damn much."

"Then come make love to me," Srikkanth beckoned.

Jaime nodded, his heart pounding as he reached for the lube, coating his fingers thoroughly before sliding them down over Srikkanth's balls to his tight entrance. Srikkanth spread his legs, bending one knee to open himself more fully to Jaime's explorations. Reverently, Jaime lowered his head and kissed the hair-roughened skin of Srikkanth's inner thigh as he circled the tempting rosette. He turned his head back and forth, trailing his lips over sensitive skin as his finger probed lightly, barely enough to penetrate.

Above him, Srikkanth let out a stifled sob of desire. Jaime smiled and worked his finger a little deeper, eyes fixed on the place where they were joined. When his knuckles bumped the curve of Srikkanth's ass, he paused, twisting his finger back and forth as he sought the little bump that would intensify his lover's pleasure. The next cry that escaped Srikkanth's lips could not be so easily muffled.

"That's it," Jaime urged. "Moan for me. Let me hear how good I'm making you feel."

"Too good," Srikkanth pleaded. "You're going to make me come."

"And that would be bad because?" Jaime asked, the words making him swell with pride.

"I want to make you feel good too," Srikkanth protested.

"You will," Jaime promised, "but you said yourself you hadn't needed the supplies for awhile. I don't want to hurt you, so I'm going to take my time and prepare you properly."

Srikkanth didn't try to argue with that, though he wasn't sure he had the patience for the long slow preparation Jaime proposed. He knew his boyfriend well enough to know that once he made up his mind, there was no changing it. He'd just have to endure.

That thought got an amused snort. As if lying back and letting Jaime finger fuck him was something to be endured. Something to be treasured, to be enjoyed, to be coveted, perhaps, but not something to be endured. It felt far too good for that.

"What?" Jaime asked, not sure what to make of the sound.

"Nothing," Srikkanth rasped. "Just thinking how good it feels."

Jaime was skeptical, but he accepted the explanation because he had far more important things to occupy his mind, like making Srikkanth scream in ecstasy. Adding a second finger next to the first, he began shunting them with more force in and out of the tight passage. Srikkanth's muscles were relaxing slowly around him, but not fast enough for him to move on. He scissored his fingers, stretching the guardian ring more deliberately, his eyes fixed on Srikkanth's face as he watched for any sign of pain. He'd rather postpone their lovemaking than do anything that would hurt his lover. Srikkanth gave no indication of discomfort, much to Jaime's relief, his body moving in time with the fingering, lifting to meet the inward thrusts, increasing the rhythm of Jaime's ingress.

Wanting to wind Srikkanth even more tightly, Jaime bent and licked a long stripe up the length of Srikkanth's cock from root to leaking tip, lingering at the head to suck it clean.

"Oh, fuck," Srikkanth moaned. "Jaime!"

"Yes, *amante*?"

"Please," Srikkanth begged. "Fuck me already."

Jaime smiled and lifted his head, adding a third finger into Srikkanth's passage as he reached for the condom with his unoccupied hand. He tore the wrapping open with his teeth and rolled it onto his aching cock one-handed. Even prepared, though, he didn't remove his fingers immediately, focusing deliberately on Srikkanth's prostate, massaging it repeatedly until Srikkanth was thrashing on the bed, a constant stream of moans coming from his lips. For a moment, Jaime considered bringing him off that way, just to make sure he was fully relaxed, but he didn't have the patience to wait until Srikkanth was ready a second time. Not tonight, when he'd already waited so long and his emotions were already running so high. He'd just have to be careful and go slow.

Carefully withdrawing his fingers, he moved between Srikkanth's legs, lifting one ankle to his shoulder and draping the other around his hip so he would have uninhibited access to his lover's body. Srikkanth moved eagerly into the configuration he proposed, reaching toward Jaime's cock, clearly intending to urge him on. Jaime caught his lover's hand and lifted it to his lips, kissing it gently, then setting it aside. "Lie back and let me take care of you," he insisted.

Srikkanth groaned, but that was the extent of his protest. Instead, he used the leg around Jaime's waist to tug him closer. Jaime leaned over him, balancing on one hand as he lined up and pressed inside Srikkanth's hot body, his gaze glued on the sight of his cock disappearing into Srikkanth's tight hole. Even after all the time he'd spent preparing his lover, he still felt like he would barely fit inside, so forcefully did the guardian muscle squeeze around him. "Are you all right?" he gasped, not wanting to hurt Srikkanth.

"I'm fine," Srikkanth grunted. "Better than fine. Move, damn it!"

That was all the encouragement Jaime needed, letting his control ease a little as he slid the rest of the way home, the feeling of being sheathed in Srikkanth's body nearly overwhelming. He took a deep breath as their groins met, trying to steady his nerves, but the combined scents of incense, Srikkanth's cologne and their arousal hit him hard, leaving him even more precariously on edge than before. He began to move, trying to keep his thrusts steady. He doubted seriously he succeeded, but Srikkanth didn't seem to mind if the way he was writhing and moaning was any indication.

"Please," Srikkanth begged, lost in the haze of desire that Jaime had inspired.

Jaime leaned forward to kiss Srikkanth, the movement lifting Srikkanth's hips off the bed and changing the angle of his penetration. "Oh, God, Jaime!"

Srikkanth's ankle slipped from Jaime's shoulder as their lips met and clung, Jaime's hips moving faster and faster until they were both grunting hard in rhythm with the pummeling. Jaime wanted the moment to go on forever, but his body betrayed him, the premonitory quivers beginning at the base of his spine. Knowing he wouldn't be able to stave off his climax much longer, he slipped a hand between their bodies to find Srikkanth's leaking erection, circling it with his fist and pumping it in time to his thrusts. Srikkanth threw his head back with a hoarse shout, his cock twitching as it spilled all over Jaime's hand and his own stomach. The spasms of his orgasm massaged Jaime's cock, triggering his own release. He collapsed forward onto Srikkanth, unmindful of the sticky mess between them or the full condom he'd have to deal with soon. He wanted to simply lie there and wallow in the wonderful stickiness, the heady smell of their semen blending with the incense, the tickle of Srikkanth's heavy breathing against his temple. Reality would interfere soon enough. He'd hold it at bay for as long as he could.

Eventually, Srikkanth shifted beneath him, a slight moan escaping his lips. Jaime pulled back immediately, afraid he'd hurt his lover. The last thing he wanted was to end an otherwise amazing evening by causing Srikkanth pain of any kind. "You all right?" he verified.

"Never better," Srikkanth promised, "but you were getting a little heavy." He reached for Jaime, pulling him back down next to him and snuggling into his embrace again.

"Let me get rid of the condom and we can do this all night," Jaime proposed.

Srikkanth chuckled. "Do you think Sophie will let us?"

"Probably not," Jaime agreed, tying off the condom and throwing it in the trash can, "but we can lie here together until she makes us get up."

Srikkanth smiled and ran his finger down Jaime's back as he turned away to switch off the light. He could feel the shiver that went down his lover's spine at even that innocent touch and wondered how soon Jaime would be interested in another round.

Maybe when he got up to feed Sophie, he'd see if he could find the stash of condoms Jaime had referred to. Just in case.

"Do much of that and I'm going to make you go downstairs now instead of in the morning," Jaime warned, turning back into Srikkanth's arms and pulling the sheet over them.

Srikkanth laughed with the joy of it all. "I was just thinking about getting them when I get up with Sophie," he admitted.

Jaime leaned over and kissed Srikkanth tenderly. "Sounds perfect to me."

CHAPTER NINETEEN

"HOW did it go?" Jaime asked when Srikkanth got home.

"Really well," Srikkanth replied, his bemusement clear in his voice and on his face. "The kids were really interested and asked serious questions about the process and the profession."

"Then what's with the look on your face?" Jaime inquired.

Srikkanth shook his head. "Since when is it cool to have a gay brother? And for that gay brother's boyfriend to come to talk to your class?"

Jaime's brow wrinkled. "What?"

"Diana came running up to me the minute I walked into her class, giving me a big hug and introducing me to all her friends as her brother's boyfriend," Srikkanth recounted. "Not a single one of them so much as blinked. If anything, they seemed even more excited about what I had to say after she said that. And I heard them in the hall after class talking about how cool it was that I'd come in and asking her if her brother was as hot as his boyfriend."

"They were raised on *Queer as Folk* and *Brokeback Mountain* and *Torchwood* and the like," Jaime reminded Srikkanth. "Being gay isn't as stigmatized as it was even a few years ago. I'm not saying it's perfectly accepted, and I'm sure Diana introduced you that way to people she knew would react positively. She never let Mamá see it, but she started wearing a rainbow bracelet after I came out. I'd pick her up at school sometimes and she'd have it on. Even before we started dating, I doubt she was friends with many people who would scorn us."

That made sense to Srikkanth, in a backwards sort of way. Even so…. "I would've had a far easier time of it if things had been like that when I was in high school."

"Me too," Jaime agreed with a laugh. "Thank you again for doing this for her. Popularity aside, it means a lot to me that you'd make the effort to rearrange your schedule so you could go and talk to her class."

"My boss was cool with it," Srikkanth assured him. "He said it was great publicity for the company both in terms of future recruiting and in terms of community-mindedness. He was even talking about setting up a work study. I could probably go once a month and he'd willingly give me the time."

Jaime laughed. "Diana wouldn't know what to do with herself with all the attention. I'm glad your boss understood, but you're still the one who made the effort."

"Family is important," Srikkanth said simply.

Jaime's breath caught. Srikkanth had made more and more comments to that effect in the month since they'd first had Sunday dinner with his family. They'd gone back every week, as much at Srikkanth's insistence as because Jaime wanted to visit. His mother and Paula had kept Sophie at least once each week and had hinted they'd love to see her even more often. Srikkanth hadn't said yes or no yet, but with Sophie beginning to scoot around, although she hadn't quite managed to crawl yet, Jaime suspected it wouldn't be long until Srikkanth gave in and let them keep her at least part of every day. Each time they were over, Alvaro would repeat his warning about Sophie not staying where they put her much longer, to Jaime's increasing amusement. He wasn't sure his brother could be any more smitten with the little girl. It wouldn't be long, Jaime was sure, before Sophie started crawling, and when that happened, Srikkanth would have a much more difficult time taking care of her while he worked. And that wouldn't be the last challenge they'd have to face.

"I've been thinking," Jaime said slowly. "What would you think about making us a family legally?"

"What?" Srikkanth asked, not sure how to interpret Jaime's question.

"I know a piece of paper won't make us more of a couple than we are now, won't make us love each other more or make me more important to Sophie, but it will matter when she gets older and starts school and—"

"Wait," Srikkanth interrupted. "Slow down. What are you saying?"

"I'm saying I love you and I want us to get married. I want to spend the rest of my life as your husband," Jaime clarified. "I want to adopt Sophie and make us a family in the eyes of the law too. I want to know that if you weren't available, I'd be able to make decisions about Sophie's welfare. I want to be the one they call if something ever happens to you."

"As long as it isn't just about Sophie," Srikkanth said slowly.

"Of course it's not just about Sophie," Jaime protested. "I didn't think I needed to tell you how much I love you, but if you need the extra reassurance, I'd be happy to—"

Srikkanth cut off the rush of words by the simple expedient of closing his lips over Jaime's, kissing him tenderly until the flow of words ended. "Yes," he said when he lifted his head, "I'll marry you. I'll make a family with you, you and me and Sophie. We'll start the adoption process as soon as we figure out what that entails."

Jaime pulled Srikkanth into his arms, kissing him hungrily, all hesitation gone now that he had the commitment from Srikkanth he'd wanted for so long. Laughing joyfully, he spun Srikkanth around. "We have to call Mamá. She'll want a big wedding. She was an absolute demon when Lourdes got married, and with your mother not around to be involved, she'll end up planning everything instead of just half of it."

"I should call my parents," Srikkanth said seriously. "I haven't told them anything about Sophie or about you. It's not like we talk very often, with the time difference and all, and I didn't know how to explain, and it was just easier not to mention it, but it's bad enough they don't know about their granddaughter yet. I can't get married and not tell them."

Jaime nodded. "Do you want me to stay with you while you call?"

Srikkanth paused for a moment, calculating the time difference with India. "They're eleven and a half hours ahead of us. It'll be early morning there, but I think I can go ahead and call. I can catch them before they leave for work."

"Do you want me to stay?" Jaime repeated, Srikkanth's answer no answer at all.

"If you don't mind," Srikkanth said, his voice bordering on desperate.

"Of course," Jaime said. "That's why I asked. Let's go. The sooner we call, the sooner it'll be done, and then we can go have dinner with Mamá."

"Is she expecting us for dinner?" Srikkanth asked.

"No, but since when has that mattered? If we don't stay, she'll send us home with enough food for a week anyway, so we may as well eat it with her. And if you think she'll let us get away after we tell her we're getting married, you don't know my mother." Jaime didn't say that he hoped his family's excitement would offset any negative reaction from Srikkanth's parents. Maybe he was worrying for nothing. Maybe there wouldn't be a negative reaction, especially if Srikkanth told them about Sophie at the same time.

Jaime followed Srikkanth upstairs to their room, sitting on the bed and pulling Srikkanth between his legs and back against his chest so his lover was surrounded by him before he even picked up the phone. "Here goes nothing," Srikkanth muttered as he started dialing.

"Hello?"

"Hello, *Pitā*," Srikkanth said quietly. "Do you and *Mā* have time to talk for a bit? I have some news."

"Hold on a minute, *betta*," his father said. He could hear his father's voice calling his mother to come to the phone.

"Hello, *betta*," his mother said as soon as she picked up the phone. "Your father says you have news."

"A lot of news," Srikkanth agreed. "Do you remember my friend Jill?"

His parents both made sounds of agreement.

"She died about eight months ago," Srikkanth said slowly. "She developed eclampsia when she was giving birth. The baby, Sophie, survived, but she didn't."

"Oh, Srikkanth, I'm so sorry," his mother began. "I know how close you were, but why are you only calling to tell us about her now?"

"Because things have been a little busy since then," Srikkanth replied honestly. There was no easy way to reveal the rest of the story to his parents, the very reason he hadn't called sooner. "Sophie is my daughter too, and it's been a huge adjustment having her here at the house."

He held the phone away from his ear and waited for the inevitable explosion. It came in a torrent of garbled Hindi, his parents speaking over one another so fast he couldn't even make out what they were saying.

When they finally slowed down enough for him to speak again, he tried to address the questions he'd managed to understand. "No, we didn't get married, and no, we weren't a couple. She wanted a baby and asked me to go to the fertility clinic with her. I did, and that was supposed to be the end of it, but when she died, I couldn't let Sophie go to strangers, so I kept her. I didn't tell you because I didn't want you to start in on me coming home or marrying some nice Indian girl. I'm not interested in marrying any girl. I am, however, getting married, which is the rest of what I called to tell you."

Complete silence met that declaration.

Srikkanth's eyes closed at the lack of reaction. "I'm sorry I bothered you. I'll let you go."

"No, wait, *betta*," his mother said. "You call us out of the blue and you tell us all these things. You have to give us time to get used to the changes. Who are you marrying?"

"Jaime," Srikkanth replied. "I couldn't have taken care of Sophie without him, and we fell in love. He wants to adopt Sophie. I think his family has already adopted her and me both."

"Your housemate Jaime?" Srikkanth's father verified.

"Yes," Srikkanth replied.

Another long pause followed.

"When will this happen?"

"We haven't set a date," Srikkanth said. "We just decided to get married today."

"We will need a date if we're to apply for visas to come," Srikkanth's mother said. "As soon as you have one, tell us."

"You don't have to do that. I know how much it costs," Srikkanth protested.

"We may not be able to anyway," Srikkanth's father warned. "Several of our friends have been turned down for visas recently because they used to live in the States or because they'd visited too many times in the past few years, but we will apply once you give us a date. The rest is up to the bureaucrats."

"Thank you," Srikkanth said softly. "I'll send you an email as soon as we pick a date. Have a good day, *Mā, Pitā*. I love you."

"Good-bye, *betta*. Call us soon."

"That wasn't too awful, was it?" Jaime asked when Srikkanth put down the phone.

Srikkanth shrugged. "They weren't thrilled, but they didn't disown me either, so I guess it's a success."

"They asked for a date and offered to come, right?" Jaime verified.

Srikkanth nodded.

"Then it's definitely a success."

"Getting a visa is always a pain," Srikkanth warned. "They might not be able to make it."

"But they'll have tried," Jaime pointed out, "and that's more than you were expecting. Come on. Let's go get Sophie and celebrate."

"IT'S going to be next summer before we manage to get married," Jaime groaned as they carried Sophie back into the house. As he'd predicted, his mother had been over the moon at the news of their impending wedding, promising to make all the arrangements for them.

"We could elope," Srikkanth suggested, only half joking.

"It's tempting," Jaime laughed, "but I'm not sure it'd be worth my mother's ire."

"We could set a date and tell her it has to be done by then," Srikkanth proposed. "If we set it not too far out, she wouldn't have time to take care of more than the essentials."

"But that'll make it harder for your parents to come," Jaime protested.

"They may not be able to come regardless of when we set the date," Srikkanth warned. "Because they lived here for a number of years, the USCIS will suspect they're trying to return here as residents, even if they have return tickets. I've seen it multiple times with friends whose parents have returned to India after living here for a time. If they didn't get citizenship while they were here, they almost never get permission to return, even for weddings, births, and funerals. It's stupid, but that's the immigration bureau for you. We have to make the plans that are right for us. We can always go visit them in India some day."

"Well, it's September now. We could have a Christmas wedding."

"New Year's Day," Srikkanth countered. "A new year, a new marriage, a new family. What do you think?"

"I think it's perfect," Jaime agreed. "I'll call Mamá later and tell her we've picked a date. We'll have to work fast to find a place to have the reception, but everything else should be relatively straightforward. It's not like we have to worry about fancy dresses or anything like that."

"Your mother and sisters do," Jaime reminded him.

Jaime rolled their eyes. "They're expert shoppers. They'll have found something by this weekend once they know what season the wedding will be in."

"Then the only other big thing is getting invitations out to people," Srikkanth said. "If we can get a location, we can probably get those printed pretty quickly. Having the invitation might actually help my parents too." He paused and laughed. "Or not, since it's two men. Unless they tell the authorities they're trying to stop the wedding."

"If the authorities are Indian, they might not realize Jaime is a man's name," Jaime said. "It looks a lot like Jamie, and I've known some girls by that name."

"We'll send the invitation and they can do with it what they want," Srikkanth decided. "We don't have to work around their schedule."

"Send them an email now so they'll know the date, and this weekend we'll get on my webcam and call them so they can meet Sophie," Jaime proposed. "How does that sound?"

"Good," Srikkanth assented.

"I'M sorry, Srikkanth, *betta*," Srikkanth's mother said when she called back a month later. "The embassy won't give us a visa. We're going to go up to Delhi and ask in person in hopes of changing their mind, but I don't know if we'll be successful."

"It's all right, *Mā*," Srikkanth said. "I didn't expect you to be able to come. I know how hard it is to get a visa with the way things are right now."

"It's not all right," Srikkanth's mother insisted, "but in the meantime, we sent a letter to Ashok *Chacha*. He's in California. You remember him, don't you? He's *Pitā's* cousin's brother-in-law, who we stayed with when we first moved to the States."

"I remember," Srikkanth replied.

"He and his family are going to come to the wedding. If we can't be there, it's the next best thing," Mrs. Bhattacharya said. "You'll make sure someone meets him at the airport and gets him to the ceremony, right?"

"You didn't have to do that," Srikkanth said, incredibly touched by his mother's insistence on finding some relation to attend the wedding. He didn't think she'd ever be happy about his choice, but she had at least accepted, it or she never would have contacted his uncle.

"I raised my children right," Mrs. Bhattacharya retorted. "You only get married once. If I can't be there, I want someone there so your—" she paused, and Srikkanth could almost see her working up to saying the word "—fiancé's family doesn't think we've forsaken you."

"They don't feel that way, *Mā*," Srikkanth assured his mother. "They're immigrants too. Jaime's parents are here, but his grandparents won't be at the wedding for the same reason that you won't be able to make it. If you'll send me Ashok *Chacha's* phone number, I'll call him and work out all the details with him. I think maybe Jaime's sister has room for a few people at her house. That way he wouldn't have to rent a car."

"You're a good boy, *betta*. Kiss the baby for me and come to India soon. We miss you."

"I miss you too, *Mā*. I'll talk to you soon."

"What was this about my sister?" Jaime asked, having come into the room at the end of the conversation.

"That was my mother," Srikkanth explained. "They were denied a visa, but she called my uncle—well, he isn't really my uncle, but close enough—to have him come to the wedding in their place."

"One of those husband's cousin's husband's cousin kind of family members?" Jaime asked with a laugh, thinking about all the people in Mexico his parents considered family despite the number of degrees of separation between them.

"My father's cousin's brother-in-law to be exact," Srikkanth agreed. "I do know him, which is more than I can say for some of the people my parents consider family. They helped us out when we first came to the States. He lives in California now, and he's not young anymore. I thought maybe he could stay with Béatriz. He'll stay in a hotel if he has to, but well, since he's the only person from my family who will be here, it's sort of expected that I find someone for him to stay with if he can't stay here."

"He can't stay here," Jaime reiterated. "There isn't an extra bed, for one thing, and I'm not sharing you with anyone on our wedding night. Not even Sophie, and you know if I'm not sharing you with her, I'm not sharing you with your uncle. I'll talk to Béa on Sunday. I'm sure she'll agree, but if not, maybe he can stay with

Mamá and Alvaro. We'll start planning a trip to India when we get back from our honeymoon. Maybe next year at Christmas time?"

"That's the perfect time to go," Srikkanth said. "It won't be too hot and the monsoons won't have started. I really do love you, you know."

"Then come to bed and prove it to me."

Chapter Twenty

THE strains of Pachelbel's "Canon in D" resonated through the reception hall as Srikkanth and Jaime approached from opposite entrances, meeting at the head of the aisle between two sets of chairs. Their eyes met and held as their hands sought each other from long habit. Only when they started down the aisle did Srikkanth look away from his soon-to-be husband to let his gaze flow over the assembled guests. He saw his uncle and family near the front, the bright colors of the women's saris vivid against the quieter hues of the non-Indian guests. He had a pang for his parents, wishing they could be here, but their attempts at getting a visa had continued to fail. They were here in spirit, he reminded himself, or his mother wouldn't have contacted Ashok *Chacha* and asked him to come in their place.

Jaime's family had turned out en masse, and Srikkanth smiled when he caught sight of Sophie perched on her *abuela's* lap. She wasn't talking much yet, at not quite a year old, but she certainly knew her grandmother, reaching for *Señora* Frias every time she saw her, and Srikkanth suspected it wouldn't be long until she managed a credible *abue*. She bounced up and down as they walked down the aisle, arms opening for them to take her as they passed. Srikkanth paused and bent to kiss her, smile widening as Jaime did the same. They left her with Jaime's mother, though. As much as they loved her, this moment was about them and their future, not about Sophie. The adoption would be finalized later in the month, but for now, they had a wedding to celebrate.

Arriving before the justice of the peace, Srikkanth took a deep breath and waited for the ceremony to begin, the first day of the rest of his life. "Dearly beloved, we are gathered here today to celebrate the union of two hearts and two lives to form a new life, a new family. Srikkanth and Jaime have asked you all to be witness to their commitment to each other."

He turned his attention to the couple. "A marriage is many things, as many as the people who choose to create one. It's a promise of a life together, a commitment to face the world as a single unit rather than as two individuals. It's often, as it is in your case, a commitment to raise a family together. It's a legal bond that provides you with certain rights and responsibilities. Most importantly, though, it's the union of two hearts, a union from which all those other things come. You stand here today because you wish to make official, legal, the union that already exists. A wedding doesn't create a relationship; it acknowledges one. When you say your vows today, you'll be putting into words the silent promises that already exist between you, sharing with your guests the emotions that already exist between you, creating a strong and stable unit to strengthen the fabric of your families and our community. These are the things you are agreeing to do by making your vows today."

Jaime squeezed Srikkanth's hand, wanting all those things desperately.

"Usually, this is the moment where I ask the couple to join hands, but since you've already taken care of that, I'll simply ask you to face each other as you say your vows."

They turned to face one another, their free hands clasping as well. "Jaime, will you say your vows?"

Jaime took a deep breath and began the vows he and Srikkanth had agreed to say. "From this day onward I choose you, Srikkanth, to be my husband. To live together and laugh together; to work by your side and dream in your arms; to fill your heart and feed your soul; to always seek out the best in you; to play with you whenever I can, as we grow old; always loving you with all my heart, until the end of our forever."

Srikkanth's eyes closed with the force of emotion that welled up inside him at hearing Jaime's declaration. He knew to the very fiber of his being that Jaime loved him, but even so, hearing it that way, as a promise of forever, added that much more power to the feelings.

"Srikkanth?" the justice of the peace prompted.

Srikkanth cleared his throat, his voice hoarse as he spoke his vows in return. "From this day onward I choose you, Jaime, to be my husband." His voice broke as he tried to continue. Jaime squeezed his hands tightly, giving him silent permission to take the moment to recover his composure and the strength to lift his head, meet his husband's eyes, and continue. "To live together and laugh together; to work by your side and dream in your arms; to fill your heart and feed your soul; to always seek out the best in you; to play with you whenever I can, as we grow old; always loving you with all my heart, until the end of our forever."

"The ring is one of the oldest symbols of eternity, of unity, known to humanity," the justice of the peace continued. "With no beginning and no end, it is the perfect whole, the ideal acknowledgment of the union you are creating today. No longer will you be two people, but one couple. No longer will you lead two lives, but one. No longer will you walk alone, but together, relying on each other for love and support in every facet of your lives. So today, you will exchange rings, tokens of your love and symbols of your commitment to one another."

Alvaro stepped to Jaime's side, handing him the pair of rings they'd commissioned. Rather than a single gold band, the jeweler had braided a gold and a silver band together to represent the two lives now entwined as one. Jaime held out Srikkanth's, who lifted his hand so Jaime could put the ring on him.

"Take this ring as a sign of my love and fidelity. Wear it always in the knowledge of our commitment to one another." Carefully he slid the ring onto Srikkanth's finger.

When it was in place, he passed his own ring to Srikkanth, who repeated the gesture and the words.

"Congratulations, gentlemen. You're now married men," the justice of the peace declared. "You may kiss."

They leaned toward each other in mutual accord, lips meeting in the final piece of their vows. They didn't linger, though Jaime was tempted. There would be time later for longer, more intimate kisses. For now, he contented himself with squeezing Srikkanth's hands still clasped with his own and knowing this was the beginning of forever. When they broke apart amidst thunderous applause, the justice spoke one last time. "It gives me great pleasure to introduce for the first time as married men, Jaime and Srikkanth Bhattacharya-Frias."

It would take more than the justice's announcement for the name change to be legal, but neither man cared as they turned to face their guests. Movement in the back of the hall caught Srikkanth's eye, and he gasped when he realized what the flash of bright red meant. His eyes filled with tears as he stared in shock at his parents, his mother in the heavy red and gold sari his father had given her as part of their wedding thirty years ago. "They're here," he whispered to Jaime. "My parents are here!"

Jaime turned to look at Srikkanth, following his gaze to the Indian couple standing behind all the other guests. "Then we'd better go say hello," he murmured, leading Srikkanth back down the aisle.

Heart pounding, Srikkanth followed Jaime to the back of the ballroom, stopping a few steps from his parents. His mother felt no such hesitation, embracing Srikkanth fervently.

"You made it," he whispered over and over. "How did you make it?"

"The visa came through at the last minute," Srikkanth's father replied, patting his son's shoulder with one hand and his wife's with the other. "There wasn't time to call. We caught the first flight we could, but even then, we barely got here. If we'd missed any of the connections or had any delays, we wouldn't have made it in time, and we didn't want to disappoint you even more."

Their presence was the only thing that could have made Srikkanth happier than he already was, a fact he related to them as soon as he could speak past the lump in his throat. "*Mā, Pitā*, this is Jaime."

"Nice to meet you," Jaime said, folding his hands together and offering them in greeting as Srikkanth had told him to do before introducing him to his uncle.

Mr. Bhattacharya folded his hands over Jaime's, bowing in a traditional greeting, but Srikkanth's mother saw no need to stand on formality, folding him into the same warm embrace she had used with Srikkanth. When she stepped back, she fixed them both with a hard stare. "This is not the path I would have chosen for you, *betta*, I must admit, but you are a grown man and have always shown good judgment. Since this is the path you have chosen, I expect you both to walk it with dignity and fidelity as befits all members of this family."

"Yes, *Mā*," Srikkanth promised, the tears that had been threatening all day spilling over finally in the joy and relief of his parents' acceptance.

"We have taken enough of your time. We have a month before we have to return to Hyderabad. We'll talk more later," Srikkanth's father declared. "You have other guests besides us."

EPILOGUE

Four years later

"WELCOME to Nichols Montessori School. I'm Mrs. Coates. I'll be your teacher this year. What's your name?"

Just outside the door—Sophie had insisted on going in by herself—Srikkanth bit his lip as he smothered his laughter. "Sophie Thanaa Bhattacharya-Frias," the little girl declared proudly. "But you may call me Sophie."

"It's nice to meet you, Sophie," Mrs. Coates said, her voice betraying her surprise at the child's adult demeanor. "Did your mommy and daddy come with you to get you settled?"

"My mommy died when I was a baby," Sophie said. "I live with my two dads. They're outside. I wanted to meet you first."

Unable to stop his laughter this time, Srikkanth took pity on the teacher and stepped into the classroom. "I'm Sophie's father, Srikkanth Bhattacharya-Frias," he said, holding out his hand. "One of them, anyway. As you can see, she's a bit of a handful."

Mrs. Coates laughed. "I have a classroom full of them, I assure you. Did your partner come with you?"

"My husband is in the office filling out the enrollment paperwork," Srikkanth replied, intending to make very clear to Sophie's teacher the way he and Jaime chose to describe their relationship. "He'll be in shortly."

Mrs. Coates nodded. "You needn't worry Sophie will be teased or bullied. We get a lot of nontraditional families here. A lot of foreign adoptions, mixed families, a variety of races, et cetera."

"Sophie isn't adopted," Srikkanth replied. "Well, Jaime adopted her after we got married, but she's my daughter in every sense of the word."

"As I said," Mrs. Coates repeated, "a lot of nontraditional families. I'm sure Sophie will fit right in."

Jaime came in just then, coming to Srikkanth's side and slipping his arm around his husband's waist. He offered his other hand to Sophie's teacher. "Jaime Bhattacharya-Frias, Sophie's father."

"Nice to meet both of you," Mrs. Coates said. "I'm sure it will be an exciting year for everyone."

Jaime smiled at his daughter, already exploring the classroom with her usual intrepidness. "They all are."

ARIEL TACHNA lives in southwestern Ohio with her husband, her daughter and son, and their cat. A native of the region, she has nonetheless lived all over the world, having fallen in love with both France, where she found her career and her husband, and India, where she dreams of retiring some day. She started writing when she was twelve and hasn't looked back since. A connoisseur of wine and horses, she's as comfortable on a farm as she is in the big cities of the world.

Visit Ariel's web site at http://www.arieltachna.com/ and her blog at http://arieltachna.livejournal.com/.

Other Titles from Ariel Tachna…

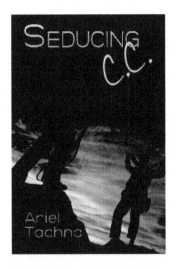

Available from www.dreamspinnerpress.com

For more of the
best M/M romance,
visit

Dreamspinner Press

www.dreamspinnerpress.com